Now It Was Time
For The Next Phase In His Plan.

Straightening his spine, he crossed the polished tile floor. He stopped behind her, within touching distance, his pulse thudding in his veins. She was picking up her messages from the receptionist, the husky undertones still there despite the professional voice she used.

This close, he could smell her—a perfume that reminded him of fresh mountain water, but through it, her own scent was palpable, and his head swam with its sweetness.

"Pia." The word escaped his lips without thought.

She swung around to face him, her lips parted in surprise. For an extended moment, no one moved. JT stared into violet-blue eyes more familiar than his own even after the years apart.

He almost reached out to soothe the frown lines on her forehead…but the reality was, they were virtually strangers now.

* * *

Dear Reader,

I have to admit to being a bit sad writing this letter, because it will be my last contact with the three Bramson brothers. These three men have been living in my head and on my computer screen for a while now, and I've thoroughly enjoyed having them there.

The final brother, JT Hartley, has been brought up away from the Bramson fortune and become a self-made man. If you've read the first two books, you'll have briefly met JT's heroine—the lawyer working on Warner Bramson's estate (though if you haven't read the first two, don't worry, this one stands alone just fine). They were high school sweethearts who were torn apart by circumstances beyond their control.

I love a reunion story, and I was thrilled to be able to give JT and Pia the ending I thought they deserved. For some behind the scenes glimpses into this book, drop over to my website, www.rachelbailey.com.

I hope you enjoy your time with JT and Pia as much as I did.

Cheers,

Rachel

RACHEL BAILEY

RETURN OF THE SECRET HEIR

ISBN-13: 978-0-373-73131-2

RETURN OF THE SECRET HEIR

This edition published by arrangement with Harlequin Books S.A.

For questions and comments about the quality of this book please contact us at Customer_eCare@Harlequin.ca.

www.Harlequin.com

Printed in U.S.A.

Books by Rachel Bailey

Harlequin Desire

Return of the Secret Heir #2118

Silhouette Desire

Claiming His Bought Bride #1992
The Blackmailed Bride's Secret Child #1998
At the Billionaire's Beck and Call? #2039
Million-Dollar Amnesia Scandal #2070

All backlist available in ebook

RACHEL BAILEY

developed a serious book addiction at a young age (via Peter Rabbit and Jemima Puddleduck) and has never recovered. Just how she likes it. She went on to earn degrees in psychology and social work, but is now living her dream—writing romance for a living.

She lives on a piece of paradise on Australia's Sunshine Coast with her hero and four dogs, where she loves to sit with a dog or two, overlooking the trees and reading books from her ever-growing to-be-read pile.

Rachel would love to hear from you and can be contacted through her website, www.rachelbailey.com.

Dedication

This book is for Amanda, my big sister,
who won't read it but will cry when she sees this.
Mandy, no matter where we go in life,
no matter what we do, you will *always* be older than me.

Acknowledgments

With thanks to Barb, Robbie and Sharon for the pep talks and the suggestions. And to Mum for the cups of coffee and the quiet house.

And to Charles Griemsman for his skillful editing, and Jenn Schober for her support.

One

As the elevator doors opened to reveal the twenty-third-floor offices, JT Hartley's heart uncharacteristically lurched against his ribs.

She was there.

A mere ten feet away, standing at the reception desk with her back to him, her bright copper hair respectably pinned up. The body made for sin had become even more lush with maturity, her hourglass figure constrained beneath the buttoned-down cappuccino jacket and skirt. The air in his lungs evaporated as the years melted away. The need to grasp her, wrap her in his arms, was overwhelming, but he resisted. It'd been almost fourteen long years since she'd allowed him that right.

His attorney Philip Hendricks cleared his throat and JT glanced over, realizing that Philip was holding the elevator doors open, a question in his eyes. They'd waited in the downtown Manhattan car park for an hour for Pia to arrive before following her up. He'd gleaned the information from one of the receptionists that Pia had been off with a cold but was expected back today.

Now it was time for the next phase in JT's plan to claim the money that was rightfully his. Straightening his spine, he stepped out and crossed the polished tiled floor. He stopped behind her, within touching distance, his pulse thudding in his veins. She was picking up her messages from the receptionist, the husky undertones still there despite the professional voice she used.

This close he could smell her—a perfume that reminded him of fresh mountain water, but through it, her own scent was palpable, and his head swam with its sweetness. A vision flashed in his mind of Pia on the back of his bike, her body pressed against his, the wind whipping past as he rode to their secret place out of town.

"Pia." The word escaped his lips without thought.

A pen clattered to the desk and she swung around to face him, her lips parted in surprise. For an extended moment, no one moved. JT stared into violet-blue eyes more familiar than his own even after the years apart. She gripped a folder to her chest and it rose and fell with her breaths. He almost reached out to soothe the frown lines on her forehead, but reality was, they were virtually strangers now.

Philip's voice came from beside him. "JT Hartley and Philip Hendricks to see Pia Baxter. We don't have an appointment."

Pia blinked slowly, then turned to her receptionist, obviously planning her escape. Since alerting her to his intention to challenge his biological father's will, she'd refused five requests for a meeting. Avoiding him was understandable—the way they'd parted hadn't been pretty—but he was determined to meet with the will's executor, so he'd resorted to this plan of ambushing her when she arrived for work, before she became caught up in the day.

"I'm afraid I have another appointment," she said with a polite smile and guarded eyes, "but if you'd care to make a time with my receptionist—"

He let an assured smile spread across his face. "We won't take much of your time, Ms. Baxter."

She tilted her head in polite sympathy—as if he were nothing more than a damn client. "It's simply not possible at this time."

She thought he'd get this far, then simply turn around and leave? When he'd discovered his biological father was a high-profile billionaire, he'd been furious that he and his mother had lived virtually on the bread line until he was old enough to get a job. JT might have made millions in property development as an adult, and was able to keep his mother comfortably now, but that was hardly the point. His mother had sacrificed too much just to give him a life—the least he could do was ensure she received what she deserved, albeit too late. So, no, he wasn't leaving before he'd had this meeting.

"Pia," he said, voice deep. "I'm asking nicely."

Her eyes seemed to lose focus and her fingers gripping the folder turned white. There was a war going on behind her violet eyes. When they were younger, she'd had trouble refusing him anything…until the end. Would that be enough now to compel her to see him? He held her gaze and willed her to allow this.

She blew out a long breath and nodded. "Two minutes. Follow me."

JT walked behind her down a hall, eyes irresistibly drawn to her swaying hips, the way her calves tapered down to elegant ankles above sensible fawn pumps. And just like that, he was craving her more than he remembered wanting a woman since...well...her.

Philip leaned over and whispered, "You've met her before. Anything else you're keeping from me about you and Ms. Baxter?"

JT frowned. He'd spent almost half his life trying not to think about Pia. At seventeen, he'd tried alcohol, then tried reckless, adrenaline-fueled sports, but ultimately nothing had worked until he'd focused all his willpower on simply refusing to allow images of her to enter his head. So, yeah, there was a whole lot more he was keeping from his attorney, and it would stay that way.

Besides, he wasn't in the habit of confiding anything of importance in another person. The woman swaying her hips in front of him had cured him of that impulse.

He shrugged. "It won't affect this meeting."

Grinning, Philip shook his head. "I should have known. A gorgeous woman and it turns out you have a history with her."

At any other time, JT would have grinned back, but not today. Not about Pia. And *history* hardly described the complex relationship they'd had as teenagers. *History*—the way Philip meant the word—covered flings, one-night stands, meaningless entanglements. It didn't come near to describing the only woman he'd let himself love, back when he'd been too young to understand the folly.

Philip leaned closer. "Why do I get the feeling I'm here as a human shield rather than for my expertise?"

JT didn't look at him. "Take your cues from me."

Pia walked through a door into an office decorated in stark minimalism. Chrome and glass, the opposite of what a sensualist like Pia should have. Which made no sense at all, so he stopped to really look at her—Pia as she was now.

Her body had ripened into a sensual woman's figure,

but she'd contained it—imprisoned it—within a business jacket and knee-length skirt. Her hair was similarly trapped by a stark bun and her lipstick was muted. Where were the bright colors? The luscious copper waves that had once reminded him of fire cascading to her shoulders? The sumptuous textures?

One other thing stood out. She was scowling at him. He clicked into charm mode and smiled. "Thank you for seeing us."

Pia sat behind her desk and indicated for them to take their seats. "There is no point to this meeting, Mr. Hartley. As I've told Mr. Hendricks each time he's requested one."

JT sat back in his chair and rested an ankle on the opposite knee. "You're the executor of my father's estate. I think there are a few topics we could find to keep us entertained."

"Mr. Hendricks informed me that you're challenging Warner Bramson's will." Pia raised an eyebrow, clearly unimpressed with his charm. "When your challenge is lodged, it will be handled by the courts."

And when he had his day in court, he'd win. No question. He'd get his fair share of Bramson's billions, but in the meantime, there were a few questions he wanted answered.

He drew in a measured breath, knowing not to push too hard with her. "How are Warner's sons feeling toward the challenge?"

"You'll need to ask the beneficiaries that question," she said, her face blank, giving away nothing. "I'm sure you're aware I can't discuss it with you."

"My newfound brothers are refusing to meet with me." Making it difficult to acquire information he wanted. If they had evidence that their father knew of his existence, he'd lose his standing in court. It would mean his father had deliberately left him out of the will. And if that was on the cards, he wanted to know now.

Her beautiful plump lips compressed into a straight line. "Legally we can't call them 'your brothers' on your say so. We have no evidence you are a son of Mr. Bramson."

She didn't believe him. Years ago, they'd lain in each other's arms, trying to outdo each other with suggestions of who his father could be—a president, a mobster in witness protection, a pirate king. And now he finally knew the truth—she didn't believe him. The knowledge hit his chest with unexpected force, but he merely raised an eyebrow. "My word holds no weight with you, Pia?"

Back when she'd been the town's princess and he'd been a boy from the wrong side of the tracks, she'd been the only one to have faith in him. Time changed everything.

Nothing was permanent—he should never have forgotten that for an instant.

"This has nothing to do with my opinions," she said dispassionately, but a faint blush colored her cheeks. "This is a legal matter."

He planted both feet on the floor and leaned forward in his chair. "Given that my *alleged* father is dead and my *alleged* brothers are refusing to provide a DNA sample, then you'd have to admit it's rather difficult for me to *prove* a family connection."

"This is really a matter for you and Mr. Hendricks to discuss and address when you contest the will. Now if you'll excuse me—" she stood "—I'm late for a *scheduled* meeting."

He didn't move a muscle. "Answer me one question and I'll leave."

Pia looked from him to Philip and back again. "I think I've said enough," she said, her voice tightly controlled.

"Any other questions, send them in writing and either my assistant or I will respond."

"One question." Still, he didn't stand.

She held his gaze but made no reply—it was the closest he was going to get to assent, so he took it. "I want an assurance you won't bias the people involved against me. Tell me that you won't paint me in an unfair light." Her wealthy socialite parents had called him a gold digger so many times that he wondered if she'd believed it when she broke up with him. And despite his current wealth, a reputation for that kind of personality could affect the way his brothers perceived him. "Tell me you'll give them the chance to consider acknowledging me as a brother without biasing them. Make me a promise, princess."

Her eyes flashed and she stood straighter. "My name is Pia. Actually, no, it's Ms. Baxter to you. And you've used more than the time I had allotted you." She pressed a button on her desk and a bespectacled man appeared at an internal door. "Arthur, please show these gentlemen out."

Then she was gone through the same internal door. JT's body urged him to give chase, but he knew it would be better to give her time. She'd had no warning about his arrival today—it made sense she was as rattled as he was.

He stood and nodded to Arthur. "We know the way." Then he strode from the room, followed by his attorney who would be bursting with questions JT had no intention of answering.

Pia held herself together as she walked through the office of her assistant, Arthur, and down the hall to the women's bathroom. She even managed to smile and exchange pleasantries with a colleague on the way, despite the sound of blood rushing in her ears.

The bathroom was empty. She went to the far cubicle, locked the door and leaned back against the cool laminate. JT Hartley had come looking for her. For close to fourteen years she'd half dreaded, half hoped for this day and now it was here, the timing couldn't be worse. She pressed her hands over her face, trying to stem the emotional tide that was rising. The last thing she needed was a meltdown at work, especially with a potential partnership in the offing. She'd deal with the effects of JT's reappearance later. For now, she needed to see her boss.

At the basin, she splashed cold water over her cheeks, patted them dry with a paper towel and straightened her jacket in front of the mirror. Then she headed for the senior partner's office. She paced his reception room for five minutes while he finished a call before his secretary ushered her in.

"Pia, how can I help you?" Ted Howard asked. He pushed wire-rimmed reading glasses to the top of his salt-and-pepper hair and stretched his arms over his head.

"It's about that matter we discussed a month ago," she said, trying hard to stay focused on the legal implications and not letting her mind stray to how JT's eyes had smoldered. She swallowed. "The new claimant to the Bramson will."

"Ah, the man you once knew."

She laced her fingers and regulated her breathing. "Yes."

"We decided the issue was far enough in the past and not big enough to warrant your being removed from the case. Have you changed your mind?"

"No, I still want to see this case through." She'd been the one to bring this account to the firm, and Ted had told her at the time that the other partners were impressed enough to put her in the running for a partnership if her work on the case was exemplary. Letting the case go was not an option, no matter what stunt JT pulled. "But you should know he was just here."

Howard's gaze sharpened. "Hartley came to your office?"

"He didn't have an appointment and I saw him for approximately six minutes. There will be no further contact."

"What did he want?" he asked as he pulled his glasses from his head and casually threw them onto his desk.

The same question had been in her mind during their pointless and frustrating meeting. That was, in the moments her mind had been able to operate instead of being stuck in stunned mode. "I think he was hunting for information to help his claim."

Howard arched an eyebrow. "Did he succeed?"

"Of course not," she said, lifting her chin.

He smiled. "Okay, I don't think this changes anything. Just let me know if he makes any further contact."

"I will," Pia said and headed back out the door. Regardless of what JT may think, there would be no further contact to report.

That night, Pia knelt on the carpet in front of her bedroom cupboard, struggling to fill her lungs. She reached to the back—the box was in the far corner where she'd put it after moving in only eighteen months ago—behind the tightly bound rolls of felt and bags of netting. Out of sight but never completely out of mind.

Gently, she brought it forward, her heart jumping erratically, then sat back against the wall, the box on her lap unopened. It was just an ordinary shoe box, tied with a narrow red ribbon. Nothing more unusual than many women probably had pushed to the back of their cupboard, but the contents were far from ordinary.

She gripped the end of the ribbon between trembling fingers, yet hesitated. What good would it do to delve back into painful memories? Just because JT Hartley came calling unannounced, opening old wounds and sending her world off balance, didn't mean she had to exacerbate the situation. But her fingers tugged and the ribbon fell away. She closed her eyes as she removed the lid, fortifying herself, then opened them and looked down.

There, lying on the top, was a photo of a seventeen-year-old JT, grinning crookedly around the tiny scar above his lip, his eyes full of the devil, his arm wrapped around a sixteen-year-old version of her. His body, encased in a carelessly rumpled black T-shirt, wasn't as filled out as she suspected the one under the suit today had been. But the boy in the photo was her first love, her first lover, more dear to her than anyone or anything had ever been…except the other person remembered in this box.

The back of her eyes prickled with emotion. She looked so young. So naively happy, thinking they had the world at their feet. So often since then she'd wished for that same belief in the world, in herself, in another person.

But she and JT had lived in a false world of their own creation.

A second tattered-edged photo was behind the first—the two of them with his mother, Theresa Hartley. Theresa had welcomed her into their small family with wide open arms, and because Pia's own mother had never been particularly maternal, Pia had adored having a loving mother figure. Theresa had been the one thing Pia had salvaged from the devastation of her breakup with JT—she and Theresa still met for lunch once or twice a year, a ritual Pia treasured.

She flicked the photos aside, gently sorting past dried

wildflowers and other tokens of seventeen-year-old JT's love, until she came to what she was looking for, the memories that haunted her dreams.

An unused pair of pink booties, a well-thumbed baby name book with a corner turned down on the B page, and a grainy ultrasound picture. She squeezed her eyes shut for a long moment against their power. Not much to remember a human life, but this little person had never drawn breath, so there hadn't been much to leave behind.

Except a mother's unending love.

Brianna.

A soft, purring body appeared out of nowhere and climbed into Pia's lap. She hadn't heard Winston approach, but she was grateful for his warmth in this moment. For his living vitality. She held him as tightly as he'd allow.

She remembered the look on JT's face when she'd told him she was pregnant—he'd been over the moon and begun planning how he would support the three of them. They would have become a family.

As she clutched the booties to her chest, holding tight, the phone rang. She desperately wanted to leave it to ring out just this once, but her more important clients had her private number and she was so close to making partner that she couldn't afford to let anything slip by. She pinched the bridge of her nose, gulped in some air, then reached up to her bag where she'd thrown it on her bed and pulled out her cell.

"Pia Baxter."

"Pia," a deep voice said, sending shivers of decadent remembrance through her body. She clutched tighter to the booties once meant for this man's baby. A call from JT Hartley was the very last thing she needed while she felt vulnerable. While she could see the ultrasound of the life they'd created together.

"Are you there?" he asked when she didn't respond.

She swallowed. "How did you get my number?"

"You'd be surprised how resourceful I can be when I set my mind to it."

Actually, not much surprised her about this man at all. "First a visit and now a call. Must be my lucky day."

He chuckled. "Still got your smart mouth, I see."

She carefully put the booties back in the box and replaced the lid, shutting the door to their past. "Why are you calling?"

"You didn't answer my question at the office."

She turned her mind back to when—only hours ago—he'd sauntered back into her life. She could barely remember *anything* other than those vibrant green eyes fringed by long, dark lashes and his crooked smile, let alone an unanswered question. "You'll need to remind me."

"I asked for your assurance that you won't prejudice Warner's sons against me, even unintentionally through your own bias, during this challenge."

She frowned. She hadn't thought that question had needed an answer. That he'd know her better than that. "Why would I be prejudiced?"

There was a pause on the line. "Things didn't end so well between us," he said, the brashness not as strong in his voice.

"JT, regardless of what you might think, I don't bear you any ill will. Besides, I'm a professional and I'll carry out my duties as executor thoroughly, regardless of my personal feelings."

Her ethics demanded no less. She had her obligations to the firm's clients, and if Warner Bramson really was JT's father, the last thing she'd want was to create more obstacles for JT. She would stay neutral, and simply carry out her duties.

"Then meet with me," he said, voice pure temptation. "Now. Tonight."

A shiver rippled across her skin. Meet with him again? "No."

"Why not?"

Because you're a danger to my equilibrium. Because you bring out the worst in me and I've worked far too hard to become the person I want to be. Because seeing you brings up memories of our baby and I can't handle any more right now. But she wouldn't risk letting him inside her head by telling him any of that.

She rubbed the heel of her hand over her eyes, trying to erase the memories he'd already evoked. "Because there's no reason to meet."

"We need to set some ground rules so we're on the same page during this situation. Meet me once and I'll leave you alone."

She sighed. There was a logic to that. She had a few ground rules of her own, starting with no unannounced visits to her office. Make that no visits to her office at all. Her bid to make partner of the firm needed no surprises, no new connections between her and JT Hartley.

Still, was it worth the risk of seeing him alone? Would Ted Howard understand that one more contact might be in the best interests of keeping her distance? She let out a breath. "JT..."

"Just once, princess," he said, voice as smooth as warm caramel.

Her heart clenched tight as a fist. When she'd been sixteen, she'd loved the way he'd called her princess—reverentially, tenderly. Now she was a grown woman and he was a virtual stranger, his saying it that way—and making everything inside her melt a little—was too much, too intimate. Another entry for the list of ground rules.

Maybe they did need to meet just once....

Dislodging Winston from her lap, she shoved the shoe box to the back of the cupboard, then leaned back against the wall. "Where?"

"Your office or mine. Your choice."

Low key would be best while she decided what she'd tell Ted Howard about this. If JT came back to her office, word would spread around the firm that she'd again met with the claimant to the estate she was responsible for without the will's beneficiaries' permission. The same possibility was there if she went to his office because it was in a prominent building downtown—a place she'd always avoided. She silently groaned. Only one option presented itself to keep this private.

"My apartment in half an hour." She gave him the address, knowing she'd regret it later. Hell, she regretted it now.

"I'll be there."

"This is a onetime deal, JT," she said, then disconnected and thumped her head back on the wall behind her.

She'd agreed to let the devil into her home.

Two

At the deep hum of a motorbike pulling up on her street, Pia drew the curtain to the side, her pulse chaotic. JT sat with his strong, long legs astride the machine as he switched off the engine. Under the light of a streetlamp, he kicked down the side stand with a heavy boot and unbuckled the helmet, exposing his hair to the breeze. When he swung his leg over the side, she pressed a hand to her stomach to ease the flutters of trepidation.

JT arriving on a motorbike, stirring up memories… He was kitted up for a ride, looking sexy as hell…. About to march into her home… She groaned and rested her head against the windowpane. This had to be the stupidest idea she'd ever had.

The bike was a different model from the one he'd ridden when they were teenagers—that bike had been scrappy and built from bits he'd scavenged and traded. This one was sleek and silver and looked like it cost as much as her garden apartment.

From the ground floor window, she watched him make his way up the path to the apartment complex's foyer and—heart lunging at her ribs—she buzzed him in.

Seconds later, she opened the front door to JT, larger than life in his black riding jacket zipped to his neck, dark jeans, boots and rumpled hair. She almost melted into the floor. He bore little resemblance to the man who'd been in her office this morning. He was more disheveled. Reckless. More like the young JT who'd stolen her heart and her virginity. She shivered.

"Nice bike," she said in a voice she hoped was casual.

Looking around her living room, he unzipped his jacket to reveal a form-fitting white T-shirt, then slipped his arms from the coat and folded it over a forearm. "An MV Agusta. Haven't ridden it in a while. It seemed somehow… appropriate." One corner of his mouth hitched up around the small scar above his lip. She remembered his receiving that scar when he came off his bike doing a daredevil stunt that had scared her silly. And she remembered kissing the healed scar in the heat of passion.

Dragging her eyes from his face, she held out her hand. "I'll hang up your jacket."

"I appreciate the hospitality," he said drily and handed it over.

Ignoring the barb about her reluctance to meet with him, she walked over to the coat stand. The jacket was warm with his body heat and she held it a moment too long before hanging it, then ironed her damp palms down her trousers and turned back to him.

He stood, dominating her living room without trying, hands slung low on his hips. "So tell me how we need to play this."

"We're not *playing* anything," she said a little too sharply, still unsettled by his effect on her body. This would have been easier over the phone, where she could have focused more on the topic instead of the tower of testosterone in front of her. The lamplight from the corners of the room added too much atmosphere to his expression, so she stepped to the wall and switched on the overhead lights before trying again. "You just need to keep your distance."

He raised an eyebrow. "Why so adamant?"

"Warner Bramson's family has always attracted more than its fair share of media attention. You will too once you lodge your claim. You have to see that if it were known we were once involved, people would start to wonder about my ethics and bias." Ted Howard already had, but luckily she'd been able to reassure him. "You wondered it yourself."

He rocked back on his heels, eyes trained on her face. "But the only question could be that you'd be biased against me. No one who knew how our involvement ended would suspect you of aiding me. And because your job is to carry out terms of a will that neglects me, I don't see the problem."

"I'm sure the beneficiaries of the will would prefer to have someone with no connection to you. And my boss is watching me too closely on this case." She would already need to conceal tonight's visit from Ted Howard—somehow she didn't think he'd understand.

"What's the worst he'd do? Move you to another case?"

"Yes," she said with certainty.

JT rubbed his thumb back and forth over his bottom lip as he surveyed her. "You badly want this case, don't you?"

"More than any other I've handled." *More than anything in her life.*

He cocked his head to the side and scrutinized her face. "Why?"

She sighed. How much should she tell him? Details about how she came to have the case were off-limits to JT, but perhaps it would help if he knew the stakes were high for her. If there was any of the JT she'd once known inside this man, surely he'd respect that?

She swallowed, then met his eyes. "Warner Bramson's will is worth billions. It's a big case. The senior partner of my firm indicated that if I carry this off smoothly, I'll finally make partner."

In actual fact, she'd chased this account, wanted to work on Warner Bramson's will after JT's mother had let slip on one of their annual lunches that JT's father's name was Warner. It was an unusual name, so Pia had done some digging and found that Theresa Hartley had worked in the secretarial pool of Bramson Holdings around the time JT was conceived. And Bramson was powerful enough to be the sort of man Theresa could be in hiding from all these years. Circumstantial evidence, for sure, but enough to convince Pia that it might be true.

She'd lobbied for the account to be brought to her firm in hope there would be something she could do to guide Warner to confirm JT was his son, and then to redress Theresa's treatment. But Pia had failed—up until his death, Warner had denied there were any other children he'd need to make allowance for when she'd probed in her professional capacity.

She lifted her chin. "I've been working toward making partner since I started at the firm—I won't risk being moved to another case because of a perceived conflict of interest."

It was her big chance. The partners at her firm had been so impressed when she landed the account in the first place that they'd promised she'd likely make partner when it was all concluded. She might have been initially interested in the case for Theresa, but now it had dovetailed into her primary career goal—make partner.

He arched an eyebrow, the trace of a smile lurking on his lips. "You've got yourself a carrot and a stick on the one case."

Was he taking this seriously? "JT, if you—"

The intensity in his eyes turned serious. "It's okay, I get it. You followed your family into law and now you're committed to making a success of it. Fair enough. We definitely need some ground rules to survive. Are you going to invite me to sit down?"

"No, you won't be here that long." She didn't want him settling in—this had to be as quick as she could make it. If she'd been thinking straight, she wouldn't have taken his jacket either. "What sorts of rules are you thinking?"

"We start with your agreeing you won't be biased against me, or influence others to be."

"I already told you I won't—" she held up her hand to stop whatever protest his open mouth was about to voice "—but for the sake of these negotiations, I swear I won't."

He gave a satisfied nod. "I appreciate it."

"In return, you'll agree not to set foot in my firm's offices or my apartment again."

He looked at her from under heavy eyelids. "What if you invite me?"

He was flirting with her now? That's where he thought their relationship was headed?

"I won't," she said firmly despite the heat creeping up her neck.

"But if you do?" He folded his arms across his broad chest and the action made his biceps strain against the sleeves of his T-shirt. Her mouth dried. His body had always been strong because he'd been active, but those arms were beautiful. She blinked. What were they talking about?

Invitations. She swallowed. "Okay, you agree not to set foot on the premises of my work or home *without an invitation.* And I want you to agree that in any contact we have—which should be minimal—we have no mention of the past."

She knew he must have questions about their breakup—she hadn't explained it well at sixteen. She probably couldn't explain it well even now. And the guilt for hurting him then still lived in her gut like heavy, sticky molasses. Delving into that wouldn't help anyone; it would only make things messier.

"Anything before this moment?" He arched an eyebrow. "What if it's relevant to my claim?"

"No mention of our *shared* past. Our relationship." She crossed her arms under her breasts, mirroring his pose, and his eyes followed the action, resting too intimately for her comfort level.

"Fair enough, princess," he said with a rasp in his voice.

Her heart missed a beat. "Don't call me princess."

"Is that a rule or a request?"

"A ground rule, JT."

"Sure," he said too casually. "If you stop saying my name like that."

She did a quick mental scan of how she'd been saying it, but couldn't see anything to give offence. "Like what?"

"Say it," he commanded in a low, seductive voice.

"JT," she said.

A lazy smile spread across his face. "Yeah, like that."

Pia stared at him, perplexed, but he didn't explain why simply saying his name could be a problem.

"And while we're at it," he said, "that chain has to go."

She glanced down at her necklace. A simple gold chain with a P that hung low. "I've always worn it."

"I know, and it's always driven me crazy. If you want our past off the table, then you need to remove it." He blinked slowly. "It sits in your cleavage and you don't want my mind going there any more than I can help."

His gaze locked on hers and didn't waver. Her pulse raced erratically. He'd cornered her with a few words and he knew it. If she refused, she'd be inviting his flirting and she was so close to doing that already that she couldn't take the risk of sending the wrong signals. With trembling fingers she slipped off the chain. As soon as he left, she could put it back on—he'd never know because she shouldn't be seeing him again. She dropped it on the coffee table.

"And," he said, seeming to warm to his subject, "you need to keep your feet covered."

Her mouth dropped open. "What?"

"You're not the Pia I remember. You're buttoned down and covered up. The only hint of my Pia is those brightly painted toe nails."

A delicious shiver zipped across her skin at the way he said *my Pia,* but she ignored it as she looked down at the hot pink she'd painted on yesterday while she'd been home sick. "It's just nail polish. Lots of women wear it."

"But they wear it somewhere people can see. I'm guessing you never wear it on your fingers. Only on your toes, and then you always wear closed-toe shoes at work. No one sees your polish, do they, Pia?" he said, voice low.

She lifted her chin, not happy with his assessment—or its accuracy. "It's not professional."

"Then don't flash your toes at *me* either."

She moistened her lips. This was becoming ridiculous.

"You won't be in my house again to see," she said, but her voice wavered.

"Even so..." He left the thought hanging and her pulse hammered with the tension in the air.

"Then you keep your biceps covered," she blurted.

"My biceps?" he said, his eyes widening.

She waved a hand in the general direction of his arms, trying not to look. "You swagger in here in a T-shirt that stretches tight over your arms, and then have the gall to tell me to have my *toes* covered and take off a chain."

"My biceps?" he asked again, slowly, as if realizing that meant she'd noticed them. Awareness flashed in his eyes. "It sits better under the jacket if it's firm," he said absently.

Feeling edgy, she closed her teeth over a long index fingernail and watched him follow the move with his eyes.

He swallowed hard, then swallowed again. "And don't do that."

"Do what?" she whispered.

He took a step closer. "Touch your mouth."

She lost her breath. He was so close.

"Why?" she said, heart racing, knowing to ask was playing with fire, but nonetheless helpless not to say the word.

JT looked down at that lush mouth and was tempted beyond endurance. He closed the last inches that separated them and brought his mouth down, groaning when he could feel the moist softness of her lips. His arms reached out and snared her waist, pulling her sumptuous curves against his body. No woman had ever felt like Pia against him.

He touched his tongue to her lips and she hesitated for a moment, then he felt her throw caution to the wind and part them, granting him access to the heated depths. A tremor ran through her body and he held her tighter, feeling her hands reach to twine behind his neck, holding him in place. There was no need—he wasn't going anywhere. He hadn't planned on kissing her, but there was nothing he wanted more in this moment. Her mouth, with its taste of ambrosia, moved under his, and she rubbed seductively against him, inviting. As he nipped at her bottom lip, his hands roamed down from her waist, over the flare of her hips, wanting more—

Pia wrenched her mouth away. "JT, I'm not doing this again," she said breathlessly.

"Sure you are," he said on a smile and lowered his mouth again.

She placed her hands on his chest, her features resolute. "No, JT, I'm not."

Body screaming its protest, he drew in a lungful of air and released her. Then he took a step back and shoved his hands into his pockets to stop them reaching for her, seducing her into kissing him again. She'd said no.

When he had control, he thought back over her words. "Not doing what again?"

"This." She waved a hand back and forth between them. "Getting involved."

Involved? That's where she thought he was going with this? He sobered. "Oh, princess, it'd be a cold day in hell before we got involved again."

Her body stiffened. "Then don't kiss me."

"I like kissing you." In truth, he'd like to do a whole lot more. For fourteen years, his memories of making love to Pia had been enveloped in a golden glow, no matter how hard he tried to stamp them out. He knew it was because she'd been his first love, but knowing wasn't enough to fix the problem.

Now they'd stumbled across each other, maybe they should make love one more time—put their past into context and take the romantic luster from his memories. He could *prove* to himself she was just like any other woman. He could move on.

Although that didn't seem like a plan she'd agree to from the annoyance on her face.

"I need a glass of water," she said and walked away.

The curtains twitched and he looked up to find a large white cat with black patches gazing at him with feline disdain. Seemed he was striking out with all the residents of the apartment tonight.

He followed her into an adjacent kitchen of steel and chrome with white benches, and waited to see if she'd offer him a glass as well. He wouldn't be surprised either way because adult Pia was a mass of mixed signals—reluctant to meet him and not letting him sit down in her living room, but kissing him like the world was about to end.

The ingrained hostess training that all the Baxter girls had been given won out—she poured him a glass from a jug in the fridge.

"Or would you like something stronger?" she asked.

"Water's good." He accepted the glass, took a drink, then put it on the counter. He gazed at Pia as she sipped hers and shook his head. "Look at us, standing in your kitchen, drinking water. *JT and Pia fourteen years later.*"

It wasn't how he'd imagined their future back then. Factor in a brood of kids, a house with a yard, Pia a famous fashion designer and it'd be closer to the truth. Of course it probably would never have gotten that far—at the first sign of trouble she'd abandoned him, ripping his heart from his chest in the process, so better it had happened when it did than once they had a mortgage and three or four children. He'd never forget that when the going had gotten tough, she'd cut and run without a backward glance at him.

He'd dodged a bullet that day and he'd made damn sure

never to get himself in the firing line again. He would never open himself to a woman—especially not this one.

Pia put her glass in the sink, then without meeting his eyes, she asked, "When did you start believing Warner was your father?"

JT leaned back on the counter behind him and sank his hands into his pockets. Probably much better to talk about this than where his mind had been going. "When his death appeared in the papers."

"Your mother told you?" Genuine interest and concern filled her eyes. Pia and his mother had been close—she said she'd been able to talk to his mother in a way she never could with her own. And his mother, who'd always wanted a daughter, had been thrilled when she'd thought she was getting Pia for a daughter-in-law. From the little his mother told him, they still met occasionally for lunch, but details had been kept from him; he knew it was to protect him and had left it at that.

He dipped his chin in a short nod. "She'd been scared of him."

Pia flinched. "She was hiding?"

He clenched his fists in his pockets. As a child, he'd thought his mother liked moving around, but in his teens he'd begun to suspect she was running from someone or something. Seemed he'd been right. "She was in the Bramson Holdings secretarial pool. They had an affair. He thought it was merely convenient. She was in love."

"Oh, poor Theresa." Pia's eyes glistened with the sympathy his mother deserved. This was the first time he'd repeated what his mother had told him—besides the few dry details to his attorney—and it felt good to have someone react the same way.

"She fell pregnant, and when she told him, he said he was already engaged and nothing would get in the way of that wedding." His jaw hardened, making it difficult to get the words out. "He told her to get an abortion."

Her face paled. "She didn't want one?"

"Apparently not, but Warner told her there *would be consequences* if she didn't." His throat was suddenly dry, and Pia pressed his glass of water into his hands. He frowned—he hadn't noticed her pick it up—but took the glass and drank deeply.

When he handed the empty glass back, Pia asked gently, "Did she talk to Warner?"

He shook his head. "She went home, packed and ran."

"That's why you were always changing schools." Pia moved closer, laid a hand on his arm, bringing all her softness and warmth to him. And without thinking, he took what she offered, wrapping an arm around her waist and pulling her close.

"You know, she never let on that she was scared—she made it feel like we were exploring new places all the time." He still couldn't believe his mother had been able to keep up that cover story to her own son for so long. He absently ran his thumb in circles on Pia's hip.

"So why were you so close to Manhattan when we met?" she asked, her voice just above a whisper. "You'd lived all over the country—why come close to Warner again?"

He shrugged. "She said she thought I was old enough to be safe. But I think she might have been homesick, and a small town in New Jersey was as close as she dared come." He looked down at her beside him, looked into her eyes.

She interlaced their fingers. "I truly hope for the sake of your challenge that he didn't know you were his son, JT."

He stilled. That was the information he'd wanted. Bramson's heirs had no evidence that Warner knew he had another son—if they'd been able to prove Warner knew about him and deliberately left him out of the will, JT's case would never even make it to court. His only chance was to claim that Warner was unaware of his existence and so leaving him out had been an accident of fate.

He should leave—he had Pia's vow that she wouldn't work against him, and he had the information he'd wanted. There was no other reason to stay. Yet his feet stayed firmly planted on her kitchen floor.

They stood in silence for long moments, JT's thoughts drifting from his father to the warm body pressed against him. He'd know the feel of her blindfolded.

"Assuming Warner was your father," she said carefully, and he almost smiled at her attempt to stay in her impartial role, "it's impossible to justify that all the time your mother was struggling, your father was a billionaire."

He'd spent several weeks being consumed by anger over that exact point. His mother had worked a succession of menial jobs to pay the rent, to ensure he had clothes to wear to school, never having new things herself, never feeling safe. All while Warner Bramson's wife *and* his long-term mistress lived the high life, not needing to work, yet having jewels, the latest fashions, luxuries beyond belief. The injustice of it ate into his gut.

He set his shoulders. "That's why I have to challenge. For her."

"But you're doing well now? Surely she's stable?"

Of course she was stable now. It'd been soon after Pia had abandoned him that he and his mother's boss had bought a rundown house together—because he was in real estate, Old Jack had been the eyes and the money, and JT had been the brawn and the spare time. He'd fixed up the place under Old Jack's directions and they'd given it to his mother. He'd always suspected Old Jack was sweet on his mother, but being an employee, she'd been off limits.

Then they'd bought another run-down house and sold the finished product, then another. They'd avoided the real estate crash through Old Jack's foresight and continued. He'd ended up in property development more by a random chain of events than design, but it was a good career built on solid, secure investments.

His mother now lived in the most expensive house he could talk her into, and had a regular monthly income that saw her well taken care of. But that wasn't the point.

"This isn't about the money," he said, wanting Pia to understand this if nothing else. "The injustice of her life needs to be redressed. She lost so much for me to have life, the least I can do is see her receive what she deserves." She needed to be acknowledged by the family whose patriarch had dismissed her like a dirty rag.

Pia disentangled herself from him, leaned back on the opposite counter and trained her steady analytical gaze on him. "You need to understand that just because you think you have the high moral ground here doesn't mean you can win."

Oh, he'd win. He may be illegitimate, but he was the eldest of Warner Bramson's sons. The only time he'd ever lost a fight was when Pia had left him. And soon he'd rectify that, too. Now he'd seen her again, tasted her, he'd have her back in his bed one final time before this was over.

Three

Pia watched JT leaning back against a countertop in her kitchen and her heart ached for him. She didn't doubt the story—she'd wanted Warner Bramson's account because she'd suspected as much. But she hadn't heard the details before, hadn't known Theresa had been told to get an abortion. She shuddered.

JT had never had much of a family—he was an only child with a single mother. Now he'd discovered who his biological father was and had two newfound half brothers, but they didn't want him. Were actually working to keep him locked out. He wouldn't have expected to be welcomed into the family fold, but still the rejection had to hurt the lost boy deep inside him.

Once upon a time, they'd almost made a family together—JT and her, and their baby. They'd had such magnificent plans for their future, but she and JT had been apart for the fourteen years since then, and their baby had never drawn breath. The heavy emptiness of grief for that little life descended over her shoulders, pressing down.

"Do you ever think about our baby?" she whispered, leaning back against the kitchen counter across from him.

His eyes widened for a second and dark pain swam in their depths. She guessed this wasn't a topic he usually talked about either. Perhaps she shouldn't have brought it up—it was too intimate, they didn't have that kind of relationship anymore.

He cleared his throat and jerked his head in a nod. "All the time."

A little part of the wall she'd erected around her heart crumbled at his admission. That wall had been protecting her from the unbearable feelings of loss since the terrible day their baby died when she'd fallen from her bedroom window on her way to meet JT.

She'd been twenty weeks pregnant and had just told her parents. Their solution was to move her away for the rest of the pregnancy and then adopt the baby out. Frantic, she'd rung JT and they'd made a rushed plan to run far away that night. She'd packed a few things together, and on the climb out the second-story window—a climb she'd done hundreds of times before—she fell. Her parents rushed her to the hospital, but no one had been able to save her baby.

Afterward she'd pushed JT away—she'd had no choice. But having him here, their both feeling the same loss, made it a little safer to say the words she couldn't say to anyone else.

"I've often wondered if I think about her so much because there was no closure. No body, no grave." Her gaze drifted to her bedroom door, where her memory box was concealed at the back of the cupboard. "There was never a chance to grieve properly. My parents wanted the whole episode swept under the carpet."

His eyes flashed fire at the mention of her parents. "They shouldn't have done that," he said, then his voice softened. "There might not have been a body or grave, but there *is* something."

Something? Her heart missed a beat. "What do you mean?"

JT opened his mouth, then hesitated, as if engaging in an internal debate. Then, holding her gaze, he nodded, decision made. "Grab a coat. I'll show you."

"On your bike?" she said skeptically, looking out the window at the silver machine he'd ridden over.

He followed her line of vision and frowned. "Good point. I don't have a second helmet. We'll take your car."

As he took a step toward the door, she held up a hand. This was going too fast; she couldn't think straight. "Hang on. I haven't agreed to go anywhere with you."

With an alluring blend of sincerity in his eyes and a commanding set to his mouth, he reached out and took her hand, holding it loosely in his. "It's something you'll want to see, Pia."

Her hand warmed from his and she sighed. After that kiss, her ground rule of keeping their distance was pretty much blown out of the water. And if he knew of something that related to their baby, then she wanted to see it.

She withdrew her hand and folded her arms under her breasts—keeping the temptation to touch him again at bay. "Where are we going?"

"I think it'd be better if I just show you."

The JT she'd known was always teasing and playing games like this, but his expression was earnest, so she let it go. "Okay."

She grabbed her bag and picked up her keys from the kitchen bench. JT had thrown his jacket on and held up the long mocha coat that had been beside his on the coat stand.

"Thank you," she said as she slipped her arms through the sleeves, shivering as his hands brushed the hair at the base of her neck before he released the coat.

He held his hand out for the car keys. She looked from his empty hand up to his eyes. "You think I'll let you drive my car? Remember I've seen you drive."

"Not since I was seventeen," he said, clearly unconcerned by her reluctance. "Besides you don't know where we're going."

"You could simply tell me," she pointed out.

"I could," he said, but his crooked smile clearly said *I won't.*

Shaking her head at how comfortable he seemed to be making himself in her life again, she handed over her keys. It was only one night, and then they'd go their separate ways. And in the meantime, she really wanted to see what his *something* was.

They climbed into her Mercedes Cabriolet and he drove them out of town, her Nina Simone CD providing background music. As the New York streetlights flashed by, she lost track of time and distance, absorbed in thoughts of their baby and what could have been. Perhaps they would have married and been raising Brianna together, living in a sweet little house with a garden out front. He'd greet her each night with the passion of—

No. She bit down on her trembling bottom lip. That was a fantasy. Their relationship would have self-destructed long ago. *She* would have self-destructed if she'd stayed with JT. Her hands gripped each other as if for dear life.

"You all right, princess?"

She jumped as his words cut into her thoughts. "You agreed not to call me that."

"You're right. I'm sorry." But he didn't look sorry. In

fact he looked more like the young JT as his green eyes took on a twinkle.

She watched him from the corner of her eye as he expertly handled her car, his powerful arms turning the wheel to hug the corners. There was something about his profile, the shadow of the day's beard on his cheeks, that screamed "danger." And she knew exactly what that danger was—not him; no, he would never hurt her. It was in what he unleashed in her. All the bad traits, all the selfish, worst aspects of herself were magnified and harder to resist when he was nearby. It wasn't how she wanted to live. It wasn't the person she wanted to *be.*

When they were young, all he had to do was hold out an apple and she'd reach for the forbidden fruit, no questions, no self-control. Her parents had warned her that she was out of control, but she hadn't listened. Her teachers had told her that her grades were dropping, but she'd much rather dream about JT than listen in class.

It had only been when her recklessness had cost her baby the ultimate price that she'd finally taken stock. The sole method available to pull back from the brink of self-destruction was to cut herself off from JT—to tear from her heart the almost-physical connection they had. Added to the grief of losing her daughter, she'd thought at the time the pain might kill her.

Over the years she'd found it grew easier to bury her wayward side. She'd gone to law school as her parents wanted and become a responsible adult. She dated several men—even became engaged to two—but there had always been something missing, so she'd ultimately broken things off with them. She might not be willing to touch the fire of a man like JT again, but she couldn't live a lie and marry a man she felt nothing for beyond affection and friendship.

One day she'd find the perfect man—one about whom

she could feel passionate, but who brought out the *good* aspects in her. Surely such a man existed?

Suddenly a familiar sign on the roadside caught her attention and she blinked and looked through the window at the scenery, her heart quickening with a strange mixture of dread and lightness. They were in New Jersey. In fact, they were on the outskirts of their hometown.

She turned in her seat to face JT. "We're going to Pine Shores?"

"Yes," he said, giving nothing else away.

They drove through the town, past the school where they'd met, past the road to his old house, past the diner where he'd taken her on dates, and then out the other side. He slowed at a turnoff to the secluded stretch of beach the locals called Bride's Beach where the two of them had spent a lot of time together. Where they'd first made love.

He pulled up in the empty, unlit car park and switched off the engine. The silence was heavy as they both looked out through the windscreen at the dark trees that separated them from the beach. A tight band pressed around her chest, making it difficult for her lungs to draw air.

Then he disengaged his seat belt. "Come on," he said.

She climbed out of the car and followed him as he walked down the path that led to the water, then turned left onto a barely visible track winding through the trees. Moonlight shone through trees with leaves that fluttered in the light breeze. The way was as familiar now as it had been then—indelibly etched into her consciousness. She used to sneak out her window at night and meet JT around the block, and he'd bring her down here on the back of his bike. They'd lie together, nestled in the trees that met the sand, looking out over the beach and water, sometimes talking, sometimes making love, always holding each other. In colder months, they'd bring blankets.

It was the spot where they'd conceived their baby.

Digging her nails into her palms, she looked out to see the view of the moonlight on the water, the shadows of the trees over the sand. The same haunting view that regularly featured in her dreams.

Ahead, JT crouched down and began clearing away a buildup of leaves and twigs from something, so she crouched beside him for a better look.

Her heart leaped into her throat. It was a beautifully carved wooden cross. "You made this?" she asked.

"I had to do something," he said, voice rough. He cleared the last bit of debris and sat back on his haunches. "I usually bring flowers when I come." He looked around as if hoping some of the trees would magically sprout flowers he could use.

She reached over to touch the cross and realized there were words carved on the front. She looked closer and saw "Brianna Hartley, Beloved."

Her eyes filled with tears and JT reached for her hand, squeezing tight.

"Thank you," she whispered, searching his eyes. And she saw something there that rocked her to her core. Fourteen years ago she'd been so grief-stricken, so *young* that she simply hadn't had the emotional capacity to understand JT's grief.

She'd known he loved their unborn daughter, but stupidly, she'd seen something different between mother-love—having the physical connection to their baby—and JT's father-love.

Yet she could see now, in the depths of his haunted green eyes, that he'd suffered a grief as powerful as her own, that Brianna had been as much his baby as hers, that the pain of losing her was his as well.

And while her family had been pushing her to move on,

to pretend it hadn't happened, JT had made this simple, beautiful memorial. The craftsmanship was exquisite—made from one piece of wood, carved and polished with love.

Even after the way she'd shut him out, he'd shown her this, shared it with her as a gift, his solace to her. Her vision blurred and she was helpless to stop hot tears spilling down her face.

Silently, gently, JT wiped her cheeks with his thumbs, whispering soothing sounds and words, which only made her cry more. His arms came around her, wrapping her in his safe embrace and she leaned into his strength, needing it now more than anything. His black jacket was rough beneath her grip, his scent familiar, his body warm.

After endless minutes, her tears eased, but she couldn't let him go. The comfort of the only other person who understood her pain was something she couldn't yet step away from. His hands made long, reassuring strokes down her back, his breath warm near her ear.

She looked up, seeking his gaze and whispered, "I wish—"

"I know," he said, placing a finger over her lips to silence the futile yearnings, then pressed his lips to her cheek. The touch of his mouth was so soft that she leaned further into him, needing the human contact, his living touch. She turned her face and sought his lips, and his hands cupped her face as he kissed her tenderly, no more than butterfly kisses that made her ache inside.

As his mouth moved to her jaw, her throat, she wound her arms around his waist, surrendering herself to him, needing to block out all else.

Yet, as hard as she tried, she couldn't block it out. It was too much—seeing JT again this morning, opening the memory box for the first time in years, the cross for

Briana, being with JT in the same place they used to come as teenagers. Too much to all happen in half a day. She didn't have anything left to give, any defenses remaining.

JT slowed the trail of kisses, then looked down at her. "Is something wrong?"

"We've been here before, JT," she said, laying a staying hand on his chest. "This isn't good for either of us—"

"Pia," he said softly. "You're overthinking. If you want to stop, we'll stop. But all that's happening here is two people who have gone through a harrowing experience together, reaching out to each other for what comfort they can find." He placed an exquisite kiss on her lips. "Let me comfort you, princess."

If he'd tried to convince her with sensuality, she could have resisted. But the tenderness in his voice almost brought tears to her eyes once more.

"Yes," she whispered.

All she needed in this moment was to escape in his arms. Moonbeams danced around them as she let him lead her to a place with no memories. No pain.

Four

As JT laid her down on a makeshift rug of their coats, Pia opened her arms to welcome him, the keen edge of anticipation making even the air feel electric. It was as if she'd waited fourteen years for this moment. Why was it only JT who could inspire this level of want within her?

He pulled her against his strong form and pressed a hot, velvet kiss to her throat. The feeling was so decadent that she moaned as he laid more kisses down her throat to the edge of her collarbone.

She'd missed this.

Needing to feel the heat of his skin, she fumbled for the hem of his T-shirt and pushed it up. When her hands made contact, she squeezed her eyes shut to savor the feeling. Her fingertips chased over the planes of his chest, greedy to make up for every moment she'd existed without his skin touching hers. It'd been too long. Unbearably long.

She'd had her reasons, but now they seemed to evaporate into nothingness and float away.

As he claimed her mouth again in deep, hungry kisses, she felt the coil of arousal at her core pull tight. Despite lying on the ground with nowhere to fall, her hands gripped his waist, holding on, trying to stay anchored under the sensual onslaught. His mouth broke away, and she used the moment to drag air into her lungs, his labored breaths fanning over her cheek.

His thumb stroked over her bottom lip and sent tingles clear to her toes. She looked into his eyes and his name reverberated through her mind—part of her not quite believing it was JT here after all these years, JT who'd just kissed her senseless. The leaves crinkled beneath their coats as she linked her wrists behind his neck and brought his heated mouth back to hers.

"Pia," he groaned against her lips as he unbuttoned her jacket and blouse without breaking the kiss. The pads of his fingers fanned across the sides of her breasts, moving to tease the undersides, and she tried to hold back a whimper of pleasure, unsure of whether she'd succeeded or not.

She threaded her hands under the edge of his shirt, running them over his back. How could someone be the most familiar person in her life, yet at the same time be so unfamiliar? Even the shape of his back had changed—newer, stronger muscles spread from the ridges of his spine—and she was desperate to know everything about the differences.

He kissed his way to her breasts, then took a beaded peak into his mouth. A hand cupped her other breast, the rough pad of his thumb stroking, while his tongue softly circled, then lightly bit. As she struggled to cope with the exquisite torment, her hands stilled on his upper back. Their surroundings vanished, all that existed in the universe was JT—his mouth, his hands, his heat. Just when she thought she'd dissolve, he moved back up her body and kissed the sensitive spot behind her ear.

"You're more beautiful now than you ever were," he whispered, then his tongue touched the shell of her ear and she sank still deeper into the sensations he evoked. The words, combined with his warm rapid breath in her ear sent a delicious shiver across her body.

She pushed his shirt up to his shoulders, watching the color of his chest change as it was exposed to the night's pearlescent light. Absorbing the vague scent of soap that emanated from his skin, she whispered a kiss across his chest, and smiled when he shuddered. He'd always reacted intensely to her caress—strange that he was so changed in some ways, yet her memories of how he liked to be touched seemed as fresh as ever.

Filled with the power of her recovered knowledge, she pushed the T-shirt higher and he grabbed the fabric behind his neck and tugged it over his head. She touched everywhere she could reach, the ridges of his abdomen, the swell of his biceps, the crisp hair smattered across his chest. The more of him she touched, the faster her blood pumped, and she felt the answering beat of his heart thudding strongly under her hands.

She needed more, so much *more.* Desire smoldering in her belly, she reached into his jeans to find him straining and ready for her. The soft slide of him against her palm made her breath catch.

He groaned and pulled her hand back to slowly remove the rest of her clothes, peeling away fabric, kissing the skin he exposed as his fingers feathered across her belly, the satin of her thighs.

Instinctively his name slipped from her mouth as he covered her with his weight, and she was losing herself, melting into him. His mouth came down and kissed her with a consuming hunger and she pulled him closer against her. It wasn't near enough. She wrapped her legs around his strong thighs, and his hand snaked between them and unerringly found the pulsing core of her, his other hand curled around her nape as his mouth sustained the kiss.

The moment after he entered her, his neck corded with tension and he held himself very still. A tear ran down her face—the beauty of finally being reunited with him was breathtaking, nothing could ever compare. JT leaned down and kissed the tear away, then began to move in a rhythm that she matched without thought.

His heavily lidded eyes were locked on hers as they climbed higher, his name on her lips, and higher still, the feel of him everywhere, and higher, before she broke free, released of earthly restraints, and felt him follow her, gripping her tight, calling her name.

She floated for an endless time, neither of them moving, as if not wanting to break the spell. Then, as she drifted back to earth and the hot pulse in her body slowly leveled, the outside world began to intrude. The leaf litter beneath their coats that rustled with every movement, the small stone digging into her arm, the light breeze on her naked leg.

And with the awareness of her surroundings also came awareness of what she'd done. Her stomach shrank to a cold, hard lump as the full folly of her actions came crashing down—she'd crossed a line. A professional and ethical line. But also a personal one…

She'd allowed herself to lapse from the person she'd worked so hard to become.

Although, perhaps it had been inevitable—a healing experience they'd both needed. And now they could move on. She released the breath she'd been holding, relieved to have understanding of what they'd done—she'd simply needed the closure and now she had it. She scrubbed a hand over her face.

JT stroked a finger down the side of her cheek. "Pia, I didn't mean for that to happen. I did think earlier at your apartment that maybe…but I would never take advantage of you when you were vulnerable."

"I know," she whispered. "Maybe making love one final time was closure."

His forehead furrowed as he considered. "You could have something there."

"When things ended between us, it was…"

"Messy?" He arched one eyebrow in faint amusement.

"Messy," she agreed. "Maybe this was inevitable, even if it was the result of getting carried away."

He smiled his crooked smile, then his body tensed and his face blanched. "Oh God, I'm sorry, Pia. I didn't use protection."

Ice trickled through her veins. She hadn't given it a thought either. Although she'd be safe from pregnancy thanks to a little daily pill, it had been crazy to do this with no other protection. As crazy as doing it at *all* had been.

"It's—" she swallowed and offered a half smile "—it's okay, I'm covered."

He looked up at the stars, then back to her, disbelief clear in his eyes. "I've never forgotten before. Not once, I swear. You'll be safe."

"I'm clear as well—I've never been unprotected." It seemed they only lost their minds with each other. The thought was somehow comforting—she wasn't the only one who was this affected—but it meant she'd need to double her guard. This couldn't happen again.

Three weeks later, Pia picked up her cobalt blue wide-brimmed hat and stepped out of the cab and into a gorgeous sunny day. Fundraising events targeting the rich and powerful weren't normally particularly interesting but this one was different. Her bosses had sent her to this charity garden party at the Botanical Gardens so the firm could make an appearance, and anything the partners wanted while her promotion was in the air, the partners would have. They themselves usually attended the higher-profile fundraisers, so she'd been thrilled when they'd asked her to attend this one with the cream of the city's elite. It meant they trusted her. That promotion was so close she could taste it.

A rogue thought caught her off guard and penetrated her defenses—what was JT doing today? Would he be working? Socializing with a date? Riding his bike? The rush of emotion through her bloodstream made her dizzy and she paused to rebalance. After they'd made love at their beach, they'd traveled back to her apartment in silence and the goodbyes had been awkward. From now on, he was merely a claimant to a will she was administering. Making love had been important for healing, for closure, she could see that, but it was over. All she had to do was hold her thoughts, dreams and fantasies in check and she'd be fine. She shook her head and smiled ruefully at herself, and at how optimistic that plan was. JT was a hard man to shove to the edges of her mind.

She stepped into the park, and smoothed down her dress in the matching blue to her hat and shoes, then took a breath. She was ready to be charming, to make a good impression.

The Botanical Gardens were huge and the annual garden party fundraiser for a wildlife refuge was always held in the rose garden section, so she headed that way along a paved path. A light breeze played with the edges of her dress and she held her hat until it passed. Up ahead she could make out women in bright, bold hats and men in suits standing in groups, laughing and chatting. She spied two women she knew from other city firms and headed for their group, accepting a class of iced tea from a passing waiter on her way.

Within two hours, she'd donated money via the charity auction and made contact with the clients her boss had told her to seek. Two hours was all the partners expected; besides, she was exhausted from the long hours she'd been putting in lately and still had more work to do this afternoon. Plus, the day had warmed—she was looking forward to getting home and taking off the closed-toe shoes.

Just as she was running an eye over the crowd, checking to see if there was anyone else she should talk to before leaving, she saw JT heading over, a slender blonde at his side. Her heart froze, then burst to life again as if trying to break free from her chest. They'd had no contact since he'd dropped her home the night they'd made love on the beach.

The only way she'd been able to cope with that crazy, explosive night was to try not to think about it. But with each step he took closer, the memories assaulted her—his kiss, the feel of him entering her, his tenderness. His companion was talking and JT nodded and replied, but Pia felt the intensity of his gaze in every cell of her body. By the time he reached her, her breath was coming a little too fast for someone standing still on a warm, sunny day, but she was helpless to glance away.

When they stopped in front of her, his blonde friend looked up, seemingly surprised to find someone there.

"Lovely day," JT said, voice smooth and low.

She swallowed to moisten her throat before she could speak. "JT." Thankfully, her voice sounded normal, even professional.

"This is Christina," he said. "She works in my marketing department." He turned to the woman beside him. "This is Nell."

Pia blinked then realized he was being discreet, just as she'd asked. Either that or he was making fun of her. She held her hand out to the other woman. "Nice to meet you."

Christina took Pia's hand and shook it, giving her a warm smile. "Lovely to meet you too, Nell. By the way, your hat is hands down the best here. I have a largish collection but that one's something altogether different in style. Where did you buy it?"

"I made it," she admitted. From the corner of her eye, she saw JT's gaze sharpen.

"Really?" Christina asked, her eyes fixed above Pia's crown. "It has such fabulous details on the brim. Are you a milliner?"

For a moment, Pia imagined her mother's horrified expression if she'd overheard someone asking one of her daughters that question. The Baxter girls were not raised to *make* things. They were raised to earn exorbitant wages—or marry money—then pay *others* to make things for them.

"No," she said, "a lawyer."

"Do you ever sell your creations? Because I'd be first in line to buy one."

Sell them? Pia almost laughed. Her job took practically every minute of her day, and once she made partner, it would only get busier. And this woman thought she'd have time to sit around and make hats for other people? That after a law degree from Yale and incalculable hours of overtime, she'd suddenly start spending her nights whipping up designs? A niggle of annoyance reared its head—solely to do with the conversation, not with the fact that this woman was on JT's arm, of course.

"Sorry to disappoint," she said with a polite smile, "I don't have the time."

Christina was undeterred. "Well, if you ever change your mind, please make sure I'm the first person you call because—"

"Nell," JT interrupted, "there's something I wanted to discuss. Do you have a moment to take a walk with me?"

Thankful for the interruption, she turned to him. The offer of escape from Christina's well-intentioned enthusiasm was hard to bypass, but there was a danger in being alone with this man. Although, they wouldn't be alone—they were at an event, being held in a large park filled with people, in the middle of the day. It was nothing like being alone at their special beach in the moonlight.

JT offered his arm and after only a brief hesitation, she slipped her hand into the crook of his elbow. "Christina, I'll see you tomorrow," he said, and after they made goodbyes to Christina, they moved away.

"So you haven't given up completely on your dream to be a fashion designer," he said lightly, looking ahead. She sighed. So much for avoiding a discussion on the topic by leaving with him.

"I'm not *designing* hats. It's just a pragmatic solution when I can't find a suitable one."

JT looked down into Pia's serious expression as they walked and wondered if she truly believed that. Had she sublimated her creative nature that far, or was she spinning him a line? Her eyes didn't flicker. She did believe it—she thought she was as straitlaced as her parents and sisters. Sure, he'd seen the signs when they'd met again—the conservative suits, the harshly pinned-back hair, the closed expression—but he'd thought it was a facade for her career's sake. And for his sake. But now it was obvious she truly believed it.

She'd forgotten the shape of her soul.

He rubbed a finger across his forehead. How was that possible? Perhaps it'd been the aftermath of losing their baby, when she'd closed herself off to him. It'd been the worst time of his life—perhaps it'd also been enough to rupture her self-image, her belief in her true self?

He blew out a long breath. Whenever it'd happened, whatever it was that had changed her from a free-spirited, joyful person, it was wrong. Suddenly desperate to ruffle her feathers, to mess up that oh-so-controlled mask she was wearing, he guided them away from the crowd, to another part of the garden that was open to tourists but seemed to be empty.

"Pia," he said, low, as they walked, "you're not this person."

Her gaze flew up to his, her violet eyes startled. "What do you mean?"

"This," he waved a hand up and down her outfit, "is one of your sisters, not you."

Her eyes hardened and her chin swung away as she spoke. "No, JT. I've grown up. Don't presume you know anything about me anymore."

People grew up, sure, but they didn't change this much. There had to be the same person deep down inside her. "You're wilder, more creative, more dangerous than this."

She shivered but her step didn't falter. "That was your influence. It was never the real me."

His influence? It'd been part of what attracted him to the teenaged Pia when he'd spied her at school on his first day. She'd been so free, so beautiful, so unpredictable.

They came to a greenhouse and he guided her inside to the hothouse flowers that scented the air with their ripe sweetness. "I think you're overestimating my ability to influence you. Sure I did some crazy things, but you were the one who had us both breaking curfew to watch the sunrise from the top of my apartment building. And it was your idea to make love in the rain on my birthday." His blood heated at the memory of that wild afternoon—Pia's hands all over him in a secluded part of her parents' garden, the chill of raindrops on his back, the heat of her body beneath his.

Her tongue darted out to moisten her lips, a faraway look in her eyes, and he wondered if she was having the same stream of visual memories as he was. He slowed his steps until he came to a halt amid lush, damp ferns, and turned her to face him. The pulse at the base of her throat was chaotic.

"It was only when I was with you," she denied. "That's not the real me."

"Then why do you want to kiss me right now?" He stroked a fingertip lightly down the edge of her cheek, and a flush spread from her neck up to bloom across her face. "There might be no one around, but it's a public place. And you told me I'm off limits. The good girl you claim to be wouldn't be craving that forbidden fruit the way you are this very second."

"I'm not craving you, JT," she said. Her voice was resolute, but her mouth told a different story—her lips were parted, her breaths coming too fast. Oh, yeah. She was no good girl.

His heart thudded in his chest. "You want me so bad that you'd let me take you here if I tried."

Her eyes flicked around their semiprivate enclosure and back to his mouth. "I wouldn't," she said, her voice heavy with desire.

"Yeah, you would. Without a second thought." He rubbed the pad of his thumb over her bottom lip. "And God help me, I want you as much."

He dipped his head beneath the brim of her hat and cradling her face in his palms, pressed his mouth to her soft lips. Without hesitation, her mouth opened to him as he'd known it would, her tongue met his, sliding decadently. A delicious shiver raced down his spine. As her hat slipped to the ground, her arms wound around his back, holding him tight, just where he wanted to be.

The heat of her mouth made all the blood in his body head south. The scent of her skin filled his head, her name resounded in his mind. Everything was Pia. And Pia was everything. Her hips swayed infinitesimally from side to side, setting every inch of him alight.

He couldn't get enough. He'd thought after making love to her three weeks ago that she'd be out of his system by now, but instead she'd been on his mind every waking moment. Thoughts of her lush curves in his hands—the same curves that were pressed against him now. There were too many clothes in the way.

As he reached for her shoulder strap, her kisses became gradually lighter. He groaned his protest, then she pressed a hand to his chest. His head began to clear from the fog of desire and he was thankful for her presence of mind—he'd been in danger of forgetting they were in a public place and someone could walk into the greenhouse at any time. Taking his cue from her, he moved to kiss the edge of her jaw, then he leaned his forehead on hers, breathing heavily.

"JT," she murmured.

He loved the way she said his name. "Yeah, princess?"

"I'm not feeling that well," she said, voice weak.

It might not be the best reaction he'd ever had to his kiss, but he was suddenly alert. Lifting her chin, he peered into her eyes. Her pupils were dilated, although that was probably from her arousal. He stroked her back, trying to bring some comfort, then almost as if in slow motion, her face was leached of its color and she went limp in his arms. He caught her as alarm flared in his chest.

Sweeping her up, he carried her to a nearby bench before laying her carefully along its length. He shrugged out of his jacket and rolled it for a pillow. Her skin was so pale normally that now it was almost translucent. He could see the tiny blue veins beneath the surface, and a fine sheen of perspiration beginning to coat her forehead. His gut clenched tight and twisted.

"Pia, wake up," he said urgently, stroking the sides of her face.

Her eyelids fluttered for agonizing seconds, then they opened revealing darkened eyes looking up at him. He said a silent prayer of thanks and let out a long breath.

"JT." Her voice was dreamy and trembled a little, but it was enough to show him she was fine. Then her eyes drifted shut once more.

No, not again. "Pia, open your eyes," he said in a harsh whisper.

"I'm okay," she whispered. "Just give me a moment."

He sat back on his haunches, his pulse slowing to its normal speed.

Any minute now, she was going to be embarrassed and probably come out swinging—he'd witnessed a momentary lapse of control. The decent thing to do would be to give her a target to swing at.

Her eyes slowly opened and she looked around before her unfocused gaze landed on him.

"You know," he said with a smile, "it's not every day I have a woman swoon in my arms."

She blinked up at him, then frowned. "I didn't swoon."

Under other circumstances he might have laughed. Even before Pia had become oh-so-proper, she would have hated seeing herself as the swooning type—he'd chosen the word purposefully. He pushed a little further, wanting to see her fighting spirit back. "Do you prefer faint, perhaps?"

She scowled and put her hands to her temples as she swung her legs down and gingerly sat up.

"Then what word would you use to describe kissing me one moment like your life depended on it, and then next you're limp and unconscious in my arms?"

She tucked the strands of fire-red hair that had come loose from her braid behind her ears. "I had a bit too much sun. It's called sunstroke."

"Of course. That's it." He inclined his head, attempting an expression of reasonableness. "Except for that one minor detail—we're not in the sun."

"We were earlier." She waved a hand in the air. "Delayed sunstroke."

"Is that an actual condition?" He bent to pick up her bright blue hat and handed it to her.

She took the hat and shoved it on her head with a little too much force. "You think it was your kiss, JT?" she accused, eyes flashing.

There. Her fighting spirit, her passion, was back. His chest released the tension that had been cramping it tight. He folded his arms and rocked back on his heels, happy to tease her now for its own sake.

"Well," he drawled, "I'm not buying your delayed sunstroke theory. Although now I think about it, you fainted in my arms once before. Remember?" He'd taken her for a ride down by the river on a bike he'd just finished rebuilding, and they were walking along the river's edge. Luckily he'd had an arm around her waist and had been able to catch her. Especially because she'd been pregnant.

The blood in his veins froze.

She'd been *pregnant*.

All traces of humor gone, he dropped his arms to his sides. "Pia, tell me you're not pregnant with my child."

Her eyes became large and round. "I'm not. I can't be." But her huge eyes reflected that same concern, then slid away. She'd wondered the same thing, too. And she was just as horrified by the prospect.

His head pounded. He stroked his fingers across his scalp to try to relieve some of the pressure building there. He had to do something, use the adrenaline coursing through his body. Find out the facts so they could make a plan.

He looked down at her, sitting on the bench. So vulnerable despite her reluctance to admit it. This situation needed to be addressed as soon as possible for both their sakes. "Are you okay to walk?"

"Yes," she said, her voice wavering on the one word. Tentatively, she stood and smoothed down her dress before facing him with a falsely bright smile.

"Good." He nodded once. "We're leaving. I'll bring my car to the side entrance so you don't have to walk far."

She stood a little straighter, seeming to have found her strength again. "We didn't come together."

"No, but we're leaving together." With a hand at the small of her back, he guided her out into the sunlight, back to the real world. "Don't worry, you won't be seen with me—my car has tinted windows and you won't need to get out."

She allowed him to lead her, but she held her chin high, not capitulating completely. "Where are you proposing we go?"

"To the nearest drugstore." He looked down into her anguished eyes and felt that same emotion coursing through his body. "To buy a pregnancy test."

Five

They pulled up outside her apartment in JT's silver coupe, but Pia didn't move. She sat, gripping the pregnancy test, stomach churning, wishing she were anywhere but here, about to do this test. Why had she thought she was safe? She'd been taking her daily protection, but hadn't considered that her cold might reduce the pill's effectiveness.

JT had been silent on the trip, probably as lost in his own thoughts and memories as she'd been in hers. The first time they'd taken a pregnancy test together, they'd been scared, but so full of love for each other and the life they'd created that anything had seemed possible. Both so certain they'd be together forever, starting a family had seemed natural and thrilling, if earlier than they'd planned.

What had they known? Her heart spiraled low. They'd been two clueless teenagers with rose-tinted glasses. The family they'd planned had become a train wreck—their little girl gone before she'd lived, and her parents not seeing each other again until now.

She glanced over at JT's profile as he stared out the windshield, his hands clutched tight to the steering wheel of his stationary car. This was an even less auspicious start for a child than Brianna's had been.

Please, God, don't let me have brought a baby into this mess.

And yet a rebel flicker registered behind her breastbone, an awakening of maternal yearning. She squeezed her eyes shut against its power. Not here. Not now. Not with this man.

JT blew out a harsh breath and pulled his keys from the ignition. "Let's get this over with."

"JT, if—"

"We'll do the test first," he said with harsh certainty, "and talk about everything else after we know the result." He stepped from the car, ending any chance for discussion.

She sighed. He was right. There was no point generating options until they had the facts of the situation. She released her seat belt as JT opened her door. Searching his face for his feelings, she took his extended hand and stepped out onto the sidewalk, but his aviator sunglasses effectively hid any clues.

He placed an impersonal hand at her back as they crossed the street, passed through her foyer and into her apartment. Despite the gesture being something she knew his mother had drilled into him and it having no meaning, Pia drew strength from his palm's warmth as it seeped through to her skin.

Once they were inside, he dropped his hand and she felt the loss keenly, which only brought a new concern to the fore—she couldn't allow herself to depend on JT, not even in this minor way. She was an adult who needed no one to lean on. She stretched to her full height. "This will take a few minutes. Perhaps you could..." She made a waving gesture with her hand, not really sure what she wanted him to do in the meantime.

He scrubbed his hands through his hair, as if waking from a trance. "I'll make coffee."

"Good idea," she said, then walked on unsteady legs to the bathroom and closed the door behind her.

Conflicting emotions swirled through her veins in a nauseous dance. Fear that she was pregnant foolishly fought with fear that she might not be. She leaned back against the cool wood of the door. Did she want there to be a baby or didn't she? If she wasn't pregnant, would she be relieved...or would she be devastated that she'd lost another chance at motherhood?

Her eyes slowly lifted to meet their reflection in the mirror, and held. She looked as terrified as she felt—eyes too wide, lips quavering, skin bleached of color. Part of her wanted to rush and get this over with, get past this mind-numbing unknowing. The other part pulled her back, fighting against finding out—not wanting to confirm that she was pregnant, not wanting to miss out on motherhood again...

And then there was JT. If this test showed she wasn't pregnant, she'd show him the door and never be caught alone with him again. If she *was* carrying his baby...

Breaking the connection, she ripped open the packet and performed the test quickly, trying to think of something—anything—else.

When it was done, she slipped into her bedroom and changed out of her blue dress and heels and into soft pants and a sweater, wanting the reassurance of comfortable clothes to face what lay ahead.

Picking up the little stick that would foretell her fate,

she emerged into the kitchen. JT stood at the counter, three mugs in front of him, eyes squeezed shut, skin pulled taut over his face. What was going on in his mind—was he sending up a prayer for the test to be negative? Bargaining for the chance to walk away from her? She bumped a chair and he swung toward her, his eyes wide and alert, yet giving away no clues to his silent thoughts.

She dug one hand into her pants pocket to stop it fidgeting, and held the test aloft with the other. "It has about two more minutes. We need to wait the full five minutes for a definite result."

Relaxing a fraction, he nodded, then gestured to the steaming mugs. "I wasn't sure whether you'd be having coffee or herbal tea, so I made one of each."

Her eyes stung with emotion at his thoughtfulness, but she blinked the moisture away. "Because we don't know yet, I'll take the herbal tea."

He handed her a peppermint-fragrant mug, his gaze on the stick in her other hand. "Are those tests accurate?"

"The box says ninety-seven percent." Fingers still tightly wrapped around the test, she walked to her window seat—her favorite spot in the garden apartment. She'd made cushions from pale pink satin and covered the foam base with a checked rose-pink fabric. She hesitated as it occurred to her that the colors were those in the bunny rug she'd bought for Brianna. Perhaps that's why this was her favorite place to sit. She folded her legs up underneath her and sipped the tea. She wasn't even sure where that rug had gone—it'd simply disappeared from her cupboard when she arrived home from the hospital.

JT dragged a dining chair over and sat within touching distance, all the while keeping his eyes trained on the clock on her wall. She didn't need to watch, the ticking was loud in her ears, counting down to her fate.

"It's been a couple of minutes," he said as he turned to her.

She pointlessly looked up at the clock. Swallowing her fear, she lifted the stick.

Double pink lines.

Her stomach plummeted and her vision blurred as she thrust the stick at JT. She was pregnant. The entire world shifted on its axis leaving her dizzy.

JT took it from her numb fingers. "We're pregnant," he said, his voice barely a rasp.

Unable to find her own voice, she nodded. Silence, heavy with all neither of them said, descended over her living room. Perhaps sensing the change in the emotional atmosphere, Winston appeared and leaped onto her lap. She put her tea down on the window sill and absently stroked the cat's soft fur, taking the comfort he offered.

She was pregnant for the second time in her life. By the same man. The child conceived in the same spot.

The room began a slow spin around her.

JT cleared his throat. "What do you want to do?"

She understood his meaning—it was the issue they hadn't once discussed the first time. And this time, having learned that JT's own father had wanted him disposed of, she knew, if anything, his feelings would be stronger. Hers were the same without question, despite the tangled web their decision would create.

"I'm keeping it." This was a tiny little life and nothing would ever hurt it, she'd make sure of that.

"Yes," he said, gripping his mug as if it were a lifeline.

But everything else would be different this time. This time she wouldn't have any naive romantic notions about JT and their future. That direction led inevitably to heartache.

"In case you're wondering, I don't expect anything from

you." She rubbed the purring Winston's ears, not looking at JT. "There's no need to get married or create any artificial situation here."

"I wasn't planning on proposing. I won't go down that track again. But this baby has a right to expect everything I can give. And she or he will get it," he said with a quiet fierceness.

She'd known he'd support their baby in any way possible. Some things may change over the years, but that core of decency and his love of children wouldn't alter. If this baby made it to term, it couldn't wish for a better father than JT.

If.

With her lower lip caught between her teeth, her hand crept to her stomach. Losing another baby was inconceivable. Her throat ached with years of repressed memories, with the self-recriminations and the grief that haunted her dreams at night. Nothing would hurt this baby. Certainly not her.

"I won't make the same mistakes this time, JT," she vowed. She wouldn't take a single risk. "I'll be careful."

He nodded. "Of course you will." Then his gaze—hyperalert now—snapped back to her, and he put down his mug. "Pia, you weren't to blame for Brianna's death."

She frowned as she tried to read his features—was he bolstering her up or did he really believe that? "Of course I was. Brianna paid the price for my recklessness. If I hadn't been climbing out the window to run away from home, she'd be alive now." Her teeth clenched as the pain ate into her heart. She'd killed her own baby through bad choices. It'd been the night she'd realized she needed to grow up and stop taking irresponsible risks. That she needed to make a break from her unhealthy obsession with JT. "She was totally dependent on me, and I failed her."

JT leaned back in his chair, reeling from the double shock that had been lobbed his way. They were having a baby. Again. And he'd had no idea Pia had blamed herself for Brianna's death all these years.

"If you want to cast blame, try your parents. Instead of supporting you, they put you in a situation where you had to escape. Or me for not standing up to them more so you could have walked out their front door." And hadn't he wished for fourteen years he'd done exactly that? "Besides, it was an accident, Pia, and you were a teenager."

"Yes, I was. But I'm not a child now. Things will be different."

You'd better believe things will be different. Forcing himself to harden his heart, he reached for his coffee again and gulped a mouthful. He wasn't a child anymore either—he wouldn't let himself be carried away by the baby or Pia this time. Wouldn't let fairy-tale images of women who honored their promises cloud his reason.

"They'll be different," he said, "but just so we're clear, I'll stand by you."

A smile flickered across her face, then left again just as quickly. "I know you will, but thank you for saying it." She picked up her cat and held him against her chest and it struck him how maternal she was with the cat. She hadn't had another baby, but she was still mothering someone.

Then her face paled. "JT, my job. Ted will be furious."

She was probably right, but his mind was already reeling—he didn't have room to sort through other details yet. "We'll work something out."

"You're right, I'll think about that one tomorrow," she said with a grimace. "But in the meantime, I guess we should start making some plans."

Everything inside him recoiled. "No." Standing by her was a different proposition to becoming emotionally involved. He'd provide everything he could to Pia in her pregnancy, but there was one thing that no force of nature could make him do—plan ahead. "We'll just take it as it comes for the moment."

Memories of cuddling together and choosing names, of buying booties and making decisions about sleeping routines pushed at his mind, but he wasn't going there. If the pregnancy went to term, they could talk about that then. It would destroy him to plan ahead, to become excited, to open his heart, and be crushed into the ground again. Those days when he'd lost first Brianna then Pia had been the lowest point imaginable. Beyond despair, beyond agony. Most of what he remembered was shrouded in darkest gray and was thick with a dragging weight that could draw him down if he let himself dwell on it.

"JT?" Pia asked, her voice uncertain.

He shook his head quickly to release the black cobwebs that covered his mind. "I have to go." He jumped up, needing air, to get out.

"Okay," she said faintly.

He clenched his fists, restraining himself from running out her front door, determined to walk out like a sane person. "I'll call you later," he said through a tight jaw and headed for the sanctuary of his car.

After an almost-sleepless night spent tossing and worrying, Pia was heading for the kitchen when she saw JT's silver coupe pull up on the street. Eight o'clock on a Sunday morning was early to drop by, but when he emerged her entire body woke up and stretched in a way that had nothing at all to do with surprise. Rumpled dark hair and aviator sunglasses led her eyes down to a black polo shirt that pulled taut over his biceps as he reached into the backseat and pulled out shopping bags. When he stepped around the back of the car, the sight of faded denims sitting low on his hips incited thoughts of muscled thighs and…

She gripped the curtain and groaned. If she was to spend time with the father of her baby, somehow she had to find a way to rein in her recalcitrant mind. And her rebellious body.

But in some ways, it felt *good* to have thoughts that didn't involve anguish. Even if they were about JT. She buzzed him into the foyer and before he could knock, she opened the door.

"Good morning, JT."

"Morning." He edged past her and deposited the bags on her kitchen counter. "These are for you."

She reached for one and peeped in. It was full of pill bottles and packets—large ones, small ones, brightly colored, some in pastels, many with pictures of a pregnant woman on the front. She looked up at him with an arched eyebrow.

He shrugged muscled shoulders. "The woman at the drug store said you should have these."

"*All* of these? There must be thirty different vitamins and supplements in there." She felt queasy thinking about swallowing that many pills.

A frown line appeared on his forehead above the aviators he hadn't removed. "I'm not sure. I just took anything she said was important for pregnant women."

A smile crept across her face, imagining JT at the store, totally out of his depth but still trying to do the right thing by his baby. "Thank you. That was sweet."

"It's part of my responsibility. I told you I'd take it seriously." He headed for the door. "I have to go back to the car for the rest."

"*More* pills?"

"No," he called over his shoulder, "breakfast."

"Right," she said to the empty room and sat down on a stool to look through the bags of supplements. She had work in her briefcase that she'd brought home for the weekend, but the events unfolding in her apartment were too bizarre not to have her full attention.

Within five minutes he'd covered her kitchen counter with eight bags of groceries and heaven knew what else. She might have been indignant…if she could stop thinking how good those broad shoulders that tapered to narrow hips looked in her small kitchen. She swallowed and refocused on the grocery store that now resided on her counter.

"How many people are coming for breakfast, JT?"

He threw his keys and sunglasses on her dining table and went back to his bags. "I read some websites overnight. They say you need a healthy breakfast."

He unloaded a brand-new juicer onto the bench.

"I have a juicer in the cupboard," she pointed out, unable to keep the wry amusement from her voice.

He glanced up. "I wasn't sure. You need as much sleep as you can get, so I couldn't ring late last night to check."

She'd probably been awake—she'd spent much of the night staring at the ceiling and worrying about the baby, and listening to her body to see if she felt different now that she knew she was pregnant. Although…

Vitamins and supplements. Groceries. A new juicer. Internet research. "Did *you* sleep last night?"

"A couple of hours," he said, placing an assortment of fruits and vegetables in her sink before washing them all thoroughly. Winston came over from his place on the window seat to join her watching the commotion. "Sorry, Winnie, but I don't think he's catering to cats this time."

JT lifted his head, his dark-lashed eyes trained on her. "That reminds me. Ever heard of toxoplasmosis?"

"Should I have?"

"It's a parasite carried by cats." He stacked the washed fruit and vegetables on the bench, and reached for the juicer. "And it can be harmful to pregnant women."

"You're not suggesting I get rid of Winston?" she said, looking over at the innocent bundle of fur who'd been with her for eight years. She couldn't imagine being without his soft, purring presence in her life.

JT squirted detergent into the sink and turned on the hot tap. "No, but to be on the safe side, I'll clean his litter box from now on."

She let out a sigh of relief that the solution was so simple. "He doesn't have a litter box. He has a cat door to the courtyard at the back." The courtyard was tiny, like the back of all the ground-floor apartments in the complex, but it had a small patch of grass and a few shrubs. That little oasis was the main reason she'd chosen to live here.

"Even better. But that means you won't be doing any gardening. I'll have someone do it weekly." JT finished cleaning the juicer, then made her a celery, carrot and apple blend. "It's best if it's made fresh each time, but I can make more now and put it in the fridge if you'd prefer," he said as he handed it to her.

For a moment, she wondered if he meant he'd be here to make it fresh each time, but surely not. "This will be fine for now, thanks."

Watching him make his way expertly around her kitchen, she had to concede that under different circumstances, she'd enjoy a regular morning visit from a gorgeous man who wanted to feed her—a gorgeous man with lean hips, a tight butt and pecs she wanted to splay her hands across. She could get used to this.

A chill crept over her skin. If she wasn't careful, she'd be in danger of letting impossible dreams of a picket-fence future unfurl in her mind.

Never mind that she hadn't worked out how she was going to tell her boss about her pregnancy yet. Ted Howard was not going to take this well. She'd need to go to him with a plan. Another issue that had kept her awake last night.

From one of his bags, JT pulled out a small frying pan with the label still on the handle, and proceeded to wash it in the sink.

"I have a frying pan, too," she said.

He spared her a quick glance. "You might have had the wrong size."

Eggs came out of another bag and, sipping her juice, she watched him make an omelet. "Are you also making one for yourself?"

He opened a couple of drawers until he found her cutlery and pulled out a fork. "This isn't about me."

"You expect me to eat food you've made with you watching me?" The idea made her squirm on the stool.

"I'll clean up and leave while you're eating," he said, not distracted from his task.

Despite a small part of her wanting to rebel at his treatment of her as his baby's walking incubator—there was a fine line between cosseting and treating her as if she was incompetent—something inside her chest twisted at the thought of this man staying up during the night to research her body's needs, then arriving early, loaded with supplies and cooking her breakfast, then leaving while she ate without tasting a bite himself. She couldn't turn him out of her home unfed.

She walked behind him and found her own omelet pan and handed it to him. "Make one for yourself, too."

He paused for a lingering moment, his eyes wary and assessing. It seemed neither of them wanted to play happy families. At least they were on the same page.

"Okay," he said finally and pulled three more eggs from the carton.

Ten minutes later she was sitting across from JT with a cheese and tomato omelet, toast and a plate of fresh fruit laid out before her.

"This looks good," she said and meant it. She usually just grabbed a yogurt and coffee.

"It might need salt," he said, handing her the salt grinder. As she reached to take it and her fingers brushed the warm skin of his, sensation exploded in her veins like a shaken magnum of champagne. His eyes widened, locked on hers, and the world faded away, leaving only JT and her and this living electricity that was between them. Slowly, too slowly, reason shouldered its way back into her mind. She blinked away the unwanted response to the man she'd once planned to marry, and reached for her juice.

JT cut into his eggs, his voice only a little uneven. "I did some research last night on fainting during pregnancy. It could be a number of things—possibly low blood sugar or low blood pressure. I'd like us to see a doctor as soon as possible."

"It was only once."

"But if it happened again and you were driving or in the bath, it could be worse."

A horrible vision rose of her slipping in the bath and falling, bringing on another miscarriage. And she wasn't taking a single risk with this baby. "I wonder how long waiting lists are for specialists?"

"A couple of guys who work for me have had babies recently. I asked them who the best specialist was."

"You didn't mind interrupting *their* sleep?"

He smiled. "It wasn't too late when I was thinking about a specialist. They gave me some names and the top person on each list was the same. I'll ring first thing tomorrow and get an appointment."

From the corner of her eye, she watched him add pepper to his eggs and take another mouthful. Threads of heat spiraled down her spine and out to her fingers and toes. Even watching this man eat sparked too much sensation in her body. The muscles working under the tan, hair-dusted skin of his forearms. The way his Adam's apple bobbed down then up as he swallowed. Her cheeks caught fire and she determinedly cut into a tomato.

"This omelet is really good," she said, hoping her voice was even. "You've learned to cook."

"I was seventeen when you knew me." He arched an eyebrow.

Of course he'd changed, he was a man now. A man whose gaze across the table held a deeper confidence and assurance than he'd had at seventeen. A man who'd proven only weeks ago he could make her writhe in unparalleled passion. A man who was staking a claim against his biological father's billion-dollar will—that she was administering. Her shoulders lost a little of their poise.

"How's your claim coming along?" she asked, to remind them both of the dangers of their involvement.

He scrubbed a hand across his smooth, shadowed chin. "Philip Hendricks is putting the final touches to the paperwork. We'll lodge it soon." His face became more solemn. "Are you going to tell your parents about the baby?"

During the night, she'd imagined their horror when she announced she was once again pregnant by JT Hartley. And once again, was unmarried while pregnant by JT Hartley. The last thing she needed now was more stress, and their judgmental attitudes and potential interference would definitely cause that. They'd have to know at some point, but the longer she had to get her own head around the news, the better.

"Not yet," she said, watching her plate to avoid meeting his eyes. "Are you going to tell your mother?"

His mother had been thrilled for them last time. Worried because they were so young, but she'd offered all the help she could give. Tears sprang to the back of her eyes, remembering Theresa Hartley's clucky excitement about her first grandchild. Another person Pia had hurt when she'd caused the miscarriage. She'd apologized to Theresa several times since, but Theresa, the sweet woman, always made her feel like it wasn't her fault.

Eyes guarded, JT gave a sharp shake of his head. "Not yet. It's probably best to keep this between the two of us for now."

Not telling her parents yet was one thing. Theresa was a different story. Even though the right to pry into JT's reasoning was something she'd forfeited years ago, something inside told her there was more to his reluctance.

She chose a slice of melon and chewed slowly, watching JT from under her lashes. Then she turned away. There was enough to worry about without getting involved in the workings of JT's mind.

She had a precious baby coming soon. And a promotion to salvage.

Six

JT walked into the doctor's plush waiting room, gripping Pia's hand. Medical suites weren't his favorite places at the best of times, but being here over a possible health risk to his baby? That had to be the worst imaginable reason to visit one. His body was clenched so tight that it was difficult to breathe.

Pia leaned close and whispered in his ear, "Tell me the truth, do you think there's something wrong with me? Something that explains the fainting and the miscarriage?"

He reached for her other hand and clasped them both firmly. The fingers on the hand he hadn't been holding were cold, so he rubbed them between his palms. "I've always thought you were perfect," he said, dodging the question.

She gave him a tremulous smile and they stepped up to the reception counter.

"Pia Baxter to see Dr. Crosby," he said to the woman behind the desk.

The receptionist's smile included them both as she handed Pia some forms. "Just take a seat and start on these while I see if the doctor's ready for you."

As the receptionist disappeared behind a swinging door, they sat on the upholstered bench seats. Pia was so still, so silent that he gave her the most reassuring smile he could muster and murmured, "It'll be okay," and hoped like hell he wasn't lying. She nodded and began filling out the forms.

He'd got them in with the city's best specialist in two days. He'd wanted sooner, but this appointment before official opening hours was the best they could do. Of course, it was a hell of a lot better than anything they had first time around. Back then, his mother had taken him and Pia to a free clinic. The staff had been nice and put Pia at ease, but what if they'd missed something that had contributed to the miscarriage? A band of steel clamped around his chest. He'd make sure nothing was missed this time. This time, he could afford the finest health care in the country and his baby would receive the best possible medical attention.

He glanced over at Pia as she filled in the forms with her neat, even handwriting. They'd talked about the possibility of being seen together visiting Dr. Crosby, but decided they'd have to be pretty unlucky to run into someone who recognized them both on one quick trip together. And if they did…

It was a risk they just had to take—he couldn't countenance her coming to this appointment alone.

The receptionist appeared again and showed them into a smaller room. As they entered, a dark-haired middle-aged woman with a stethoscope around her neck greeted them and asked them to take a seat.

"Thank you for seeing us on short notice," he said.

Dr. Crosby smiled. "You're a very persuasive man, Mr. Hartley," she murmured and shook his hand. She turned a beautiful smile on Pia. "Ms. Baxter, I see you've finished the forms Amy gave you."

Pia handed over the paperwork. "Please, call me Pia."

Dr. Crosby scanned the forms, then frowned and pursed her lips. "This is your second pregnancy, Pia?"

"Yes. I... Yes," she said, her voice drying up. JT squeezed her hand.

"You lost that baby?" the doctor asked gently.

JT smoothly cut in so Pia didn't have to explain. "Pia had an accident when she was about halfway through that pregnancy. She fell from a window."

"I see." Dr. Crosby turned to Pia with compassion in her eyes and asked detailed questions. He watched Pia answer in a low voice, her eyes downcast, and he wished he could spare her these questions, too.

"With your permission," Dr. Crosby said, typing something into her computer, "I'd like to request a copy of your hospital records for review. I want to make sure I have as much information as possible so that we know what we're dealing with."

"Of course," Pia said.

"I'll get Amy to organize a letter for you to sign. Now, you said you had a fainting spell?"

Pia nodded. "My blood pressure is normally on the low side, and I had troubles with it early in my first pregnancy."

"She fainted once then, too," JT said. That day down by the river, he'd come close to panic. He'd had no idea what to do and had never been so happy to see someone open their eyes again.

"Okay," the doctor said, standing, "let's get you on the scales, then into a gown for the exam. We'll do a urine test to confirm the pregnancy, too."

He gave Pia's hand a final squeeze as she put her handbag on the floor and slipped away. Her eyes were too large—her fears written plainly on her face.

The doctor made a quick note on her computer and followed Pia behind the curtain.

Left alone, he looked around the pale blue room and tried to relax his shoulders, but the weight bearing down on them was too heavy to allow it. He would do everything in his power for this baby, but that guaranteed nothing—with a pregnancy, Mother Nature was in charge and he hated ceding control to anyone or anything, including nature herself.

And even if this baby lived to be born, then what? Fourteen years ago, he'd thought he'd known how things would play out. Even after Brianna died, he'd thought he and Pia would still have each other. Maybe one day start a family again. Not to replace Brianna, but new additions to their family unit. They could have waited until they were financially stable, had their own house. But it had never occurred to him that he and Pia wouldn't be together. Fool that he was, he'd imagined they'd grow old side by side.

They'd made private vows to each other under the moonlight, words that had been sacred to him. Yet at the moment they'd needed each other the most, Pia had broken her promises and abandoned him.

No matter what happened now, how much it felt like they were on the same team, he'd *never* forget that she might cut and run when the going got tough. He couldn't depend on her, couldn't trust her.

But he would be here for her while she carried his child.

The curtain rustled and the doctor appeared, Pia soon

after, and something in his chest eased a bit to have her back beside him, where he had some illusion of control of the situation. He gave her a tight smile which she returned as she sat back in the chair beside him.

Dr. Crosby made a few notes before looking up and smiling. "You seem in good health, Pia. We'll send these blood samples off for testing, but I suspect because you said your blood pressure is on the low side, your fainting was a result of that. It's a little low now, but nothing alarming."

Pia shifted in her seat, her fingers knotted together. "But is it safe for the baby?"

"Low blood pressure is less of a risk than high blood pressure. I'm hopeful that yours will come into a more normal range in the second trimester. But for now, there are some measures I want you to take. Drink lots of fluids, especially water. Avoid standing for prolonged periods, particularly when it's hot. And I want you to start on a regular program of exercise."

JT looked from one woman to the other, imagining Pia fainting while she was out jogging or playing sport. "Exercise? Won't that put the baby at greater risk?"

"I'm not talking marathons here." The doctor turned to Pia. "Gentle exercise will help you prevent episodes of low blood pressure." She handed them a sheet of paper. "Here are some more ideas."

Unsatisfied with the answers and fighting the urge to wrap Pia and the baby in a nice thick layer of cotton wool, JT frowned. "What if she faints again when she's driving or on a stairwell?"

Dr. Crosby turned back to him. "There's no reason to expect more fainting. Keep an eye on it and feel free to call me if you have any concerns."

That was it? He leaned forward in his chair. Sure, he

knew he couldn't expect Pia to be confined to bed rest for the next eight months, but to have her continue as normal?

He pinned the doctor with a stare. "How exactly will we keep an eye on it?"

"You can buy a home blood pressure monitor," she said, turning to Pia. "Take it twice a day and keep a record." She reached to some shelves above her head and extracted a pamphlet. "This has the healthy range that we're aiming for."

JT scanned the slip of paper over Pia's shoulder. "And we'll ring you if it's out of this range?"

"Absolutely," Dr. Crosby said. "Otherwise, I'll see you at your next appointment. You can make one with Amy on the way out. Oh, and don't forget to sign the letter so I can access your medical history, Pia."

They thanked her and made a new appointment with the receptionist, then headed for his car. Something insistent gnawed in his gut. It'd all seemed too easy, too low-key. Or was it just that he was expecting the worst? That his baby wouldn't make it.

With his body braced as if expecting a blow, he drove Pia back to her place in time for them both to get to work—after a quick detour to pick up a blood pressure monitor.

Barely two hours later, Pia stood in Ted Howard's reception area, palms sweating. He'd been held up in a meeting, leaving her here, becoming progressively more anxious.

As she paced from one side of the room to the other for the tenth time, the senior partner walked through from the hall, folders under his arm, greeting his secretary and indicating with an incline of his head for Pia to follow.

She walked into his office behind him, taking rigid steps. Having an unblemished record at the firm had been a source of pride, and she was about to blow it. More than blow it—she was about to obliterate it. Nausea that had nothing to do with morning sickness roiled in her belly.

"I have about three minutes," he said as he closed the door behind her. "What can I do for you?"

She took a deep breath, then let it out in a controlled stream. "There's something I need to tell you."

"Go ahead," he said, his back to her as he stacked the folders he'd carried.

Saying the words to *anyone* this early in the pregnancy—where there was a risk of the unthinkable happening—would be grueling, but ethically she had no choice but to confess to her boss. She moistened her lips and raised her chin.

"I'm pregnant."

He turned around slowly, clearly surprised. Though she'd expected surprise, since she'd never once shown any signs of interest in marriage or family life. It was his next reaction that mattered most.

"Congratulations," he said, with a distant smile, clearly calculating the impact on the firm, on her cases in several months' time.

"Thank you." She laced her fingers together behind her back and stood straighter. "But there's more."

He raised an eyebrow. "Go on."

"The father is JT Hartley." She said the words short and sharp, then braced herself for his response, expecting the worst, hoping for the best.

Ted's eyes widened, then narrowed as he sat on the edge of his desk. "Let me get this straight...you're carrying the child of a man who's lodging a claim against one of the firm's biggest estates? The estate you're administering?"

She closed her eyes for a long moment. Hearing the words aloud made the situation become the awful reality she'd been trying to deny. And yet, as bad as being pregnant with JT's baby was for her professionally, it was worse personally. The only positive was the tiny life in her womb—her son or daughter.

She resisted placing a hand over her stomach as she faced the consequences of her actions. "Yes."

"You were supposed to keep me updated," he said as storm clouds gathered in his eyes. "It seems you missed informing me about at least one important meeting." He shook his head. "Why would you put everything you've worked for at risk?"

She bit down on her lip. Ted Howard had been her champion in the firm almost from the first—he'd taken her under his wing and nurtured her career. She knew he'd be disappointed in her and that knowledge tore right into her solar plexus. "I'm sorry, Ted."

"Tell me this hasn't been going on the whole time."

Regardless of how much it made her squirm to provide details, he deserved the information. "The day he came to the office, I saw him after work. It was only the one day."

"Ah, Pia," he said, shaking his head. "You know I have to take you off the Bramson estate case."

Her stomach swooped as her fears burst to Technicolor life. "I understand, Ted, but I have some alternatives we could discuss. Other ways I can prove I'm still the best person for the promotion. That partnership means the world to me."

"You still want the partnership now you're going to be a mother?"

A little voice at the back of her mind had been asking her the same question. She ignored it—when she came back from maternity leave, there would be options like nannies and flextime. She and the baby would cope just fine.

She looked Ted squarely in the eye, her hands clenched into fists to stop them trembling. "One hundred percent."

He sighed and went around his desk to sit heavily in the high-backed chair. "I've made no secret of the fact that you were my preference for the next partner. Your ability and dedication to the job have always surpassed any other lawyer in the running. But I have to tell you, I'm questioning your commitment right now."

"I can assure you, my dedication to this firm is still strong," she said quickly, lacing the words with as much certainty as she could muster.

"You slept with a claimant to a will you were administering, Ms. Baxter."

It was only the truth, but the accusation hit her like a blow and she steadied herself before replying. "I won't make another mistake. I give you my word."

His gaze rested heavily on her for long moments, then he sighed. "Tell me about your alternatives."

She stood straighter. "Linda Adams takes over the case. I'll assist her because I have the history with the estate and heirs, but she'll be the lead. In exchange I'll take something from Linda's caseload to free her up."

Ted drummed his fingers on his desk and looked intently at her. "I might regret this, but if you can promise there won't be even a whiff of a mistake, not even a spelling error on the paperwork, and if you impress me on the rest of the cases you have, you'll still be in the running for the partnership."

"Thank you, Ted." She swallowed the emotion that lodged in her throat over the fact that he was giving her a second chance. "I won't let you down."

He pulled wire-rimmed glasses from his breast pocket. "I hope for your sake—and the firm's—that you don't," he said and went back to his work.

* * *

Pia picked up the mint-green booties from the stand in the exclusive baby store and smiled. Seeing the pink lines on the pregnancy test had been a shock, but now that she'd had five days to assimilate, she loved this little person with everything in her heart. She hadn't been sure she could open her heart to a baby again, but she'd soon realized that loving him or her was the most natural thing in the world.

As she reached for a pale lemon pair, a wave of nausea crept up and she stilled to let it pass. Instead, the booties blurred before her eyes and the room began to swim. Panic flared as she realized her blood pressure must have dropped. She couldn't faint—not here. She crouched down on the floor, trying to remember the position she needed to be in to stave off a faint, lowering her head to her knees, but suffocating blackness descended.

She woke on the floor, a roll of something soft under her head, a woman above her who looked on the edge of panic.

"Honey, are you all right? Can I call someone?"

Pia closed her eyes and swallowed a couple of times to get her voice to work. Without thinking, she said, "JT. Call JT."

She heard muffled sounds that she assumed was the sales assistant going through her handbag to find JT's number in her phone. Then she was vaguely aware of a conversation a little distance away.

Despite being groggy, she struggled to sit up, but the woman came back and said, "No need to get up. Your man said he'd be here in a matter of minutes. He said we shouldn't move you."

"But I'm fine." Except for the fuzziness and a bit of bruising that would surely come through on the aching spots where she'd landed. But she wanted to get up from the shop floor.

Then in a blinding flash, it hit her—she'd fallen. *The baby.* Her pulse spiked and suddenly she was wide awake. Her hands went to her stomach but it felt the same as always. With her eyes squeezed shut, she momentarily laid her head back on the soft roll. Then she heard loud, sharp footsteps enter the store and she opened her eyes to find JT leaning over her.

"I'm here, Pia. You're fine." His voice was calm, assured, if a little out of breath.

"I know," she said because she wanted to get up, but a small flame lit inside her and glowed. JT was here—he'd fix things, keep her and their baby safe.

"Are you hurting anywhere?" He smoothed the hair back from her face. He was so close that she could smell the unmistakable scent of him and in that moment she wished they had the type of relationship that would allow her to reach up and wrap her arms around his neck, allow him to press a kiss to her lips, to take comfort from his strength.

He was scanning her face, waiting for her to reply, so she pulled her lips wide in what she hoped would be a smile. "My head was a little fuzzy, but it's clearing now." It was the truth—there was nothing wrong with her, she was sure of it. But what about her baby? Had it been hurt when she fell?

He inched his hands under her shoulders and knees and lifted her in his arms. "Have you got a chair out back?" he asked the other woman.

"I can walk," Pia said, but no one was listening. A couple of browsers were surreptitiously watching the commotion while looking at baby bonnets, but this sales assistant had all her attention on JT and his instructions. JT had always inspired that kind of focus in women.

"Follow me," the sales assistant said as she walked ahead. "We have a small staff room out here."

Once through the doorway, he gently sat Pia in a plastic chair and she looked up into his eyes, luminescent green with his intensity. "You got here so quickly."

"I was inspecting a building on the next block, so I walked." She suspected he'd run the distance from the sheen of perspiration on his forehead, but his features were controlled and gave nothing away.

"I really am okay," she repeated, embarrassed by the fuss. All she cared about was her baby. What had the first signs been of the miscarriage after she'd fallen at sixteen? Bleeding? She dug deep and dredged up memories of that sickening night. No, the cramps had come before bleeding. Mentally scanning her abdomen, she checked for twinges and found none. How soon had they started last time? She couldn't remember.

JT passed her a glass of water and she sipped, still trying to find the information in her memory banks.

"Have you got something sweet?" JT said over his shoulder.

The sales assistant appeared with a jar of candies. "We have these. You folks okay if I leave you for a few minutes?"

"We'll be fine. Thanks for calling me." He unwrapped a candy and passed it to Pia. "How are you feeling?"

"A little sheepish for causing all the fuss," she said, her voice unsteady. "And I'll have some bruises tomorrow, but I'm fine." As long as she didn't start cramping. She pressed clammy hands to her stomach. "JT, the baby—"

"I'm taking you to Dr. Crosby's office. I'll call on the way."

The relief of having someone take charge when she felt too fragile for the role was immense. "Thank you," she whispered.

You'll be fine, little one. Don't give up.

He supported her weight with an arm around her waist as they walked out the front door and hailed a cab. His lean, muscled form was so strong, so reassuring against her that she melted into him. As soon as they were in, he punched in a number on his cell, explained their situation to the person on the other end, and told them they were on their way.

He hung up, slipped the phone into his pocket and turned to her. "The receptionist says Dr. Crosby was about to leave for her hospital rounds, but she'll wait till we get there."

Pia sent up a silent prayer of thanks, and another that her baby would be unharmed. JT sat beside her on the cab's vinyl backseat, his arm loosely around her shoulders, his face turned to the passing scenery. What was running through his mind? Did he have the same bone-deep terror that she would lose the baby? Did he blame her? She clenched her fists tight and turned away to her own window.

When they reached the medical suites, the receptionist ushered them straight in.

Dr. Crosby was calm and reassuring as she did the examination. Once they were sitting at her desk again with JT, the doctor made some notes, then turned to them.

"I can't find any signs to indicate a problem. You're in the first trimester and the baby is well insulated in your womb at the moment, but if you have any spotting or cramping, call me immediately and get to a hospital."

"Do you think that's likely?" JT asked, his voice grave,

and Pia was glad he'd asked the question that had been on the tip of her tongue.

"It's hard to say," Dr. Crosby replied. "Occasionally these things surprise me, but I'd say you should be safe because it wasn't a heavy fall and everything looks fine."

Pia let out a pent-up breath that felt like every last bit of air in her lungs escaped. Her baby should be fine. She smiled at JT, giddy with relief.

"This might be a good time to discuss your first pregnancy, Pia." Dr. Crosby laid a hand flat on the desk and her expression grew solemn. "I've reviewed your medical records—the trauma you suffered from your fall caused a placental abruption. This means you do have an increased risk of the problem reoccurring—probably about a ten-percent risk. I don't want you to worry unduly but it is important that you take extra care."

Any traces of relief Pia had felt vanished as Dr. Crosby's words slapped her in the face. "Is there anything we can do to keep my…our baby safer?" she whispered.

"Keep up with the suggestions I gave you last time, like having enough fluids. And you need to get plenty of sleep. And because you've fainted twice, you might want to put some precautions in place until we see how your blood pressure responds in your second trimester."

"Precautions?" JT said from beside her. His body stiffened and tension radiated from him.

Dr. Crosby smiled kindly. "Simple things—for instance, when you're showering, you should make sure the water isn't too hot, perhaps have a shower stool so you can sit down. Try to take showers when there's someone else around."

Her fingers wrapped around each other tightly. She'd lived alone since moving out of her college dorm—how was it possible to have someone around when she showered? She licked dry lips and decided to work that out later. In the meantime, there was another issue. "What about my job?"

"That's entirely up to you," Dr. Crosby replied. "It depends on whether you feel safe there. Also, we want you to keep your stress level under control because of the potential effects it could have on your system." She looked down at her notes. "You're a lawyer, aren't you?"

"Yes."

"Is it mainly desk work?"

Meetings and appointments off-premises were fairly regular, but she could try to rearrange things to stay in her own office each day. "I can probably make it a desk job for the short term."

"It should be no riskier than being at home, but it's hard for me to make that judgment without knowing the details of your schedule. Although something to consider is that your stress will adversely affect the baby, so we want you to be safe *and* to have you feel safe. You certainly don't have to stop working, but maybe you could take steps to balance your load. Only you know if the stress you're under now is too much. But keep in mind that if you have an episode of low blood pressure, you'll need to feel comfortable about managing that by lying down or at least putting your head down."

Dr. Crosby's words replayed in Pia's mind during the cab ride home. Precautions needed to be put into place, no question, but how many? How much was enough? She desperately wanted the partnership at her firm, but never at the risk of losing another baby.

She laid her head back on the headrest behind her and closed her eyes. Four weeks ago, JT had been a distant memory and the partnership had been the most important thing in her future. Too much had changed too fast.

The cab pulled up in front of her apartment and JT paid the driver and followed her in without invitation. Which pretty much summed up their situation now—JT looking after things and being an unquestioned part of her life. And every time he came here, or they were out together, they ran the risk of being seen, of her career exploding in her face. Everything was spinning out of control, and in the midst of the mess, she had to ensure that keeping emotional distance from JT remained a priority. She would soon be a mother, and needed to keep her head straight, to be the strongest and best version of herself for the baby's sake. JT and keeping her head straight were not compatible.

He stood before her, dominating her living room, strong hands on his lean hips. "What will you do about your job?"

"Take time off," she said. She'd turned the elements of the problem over and over on the ride home, looking from all angles, searching for a solution that would suit all her needs. But ultimately—no matter how small the risk her job was to her baby—there was only one plan she could live with. "It's not just the work but the commute, too."

He cocked his head to the side, his eyes intent on her face. "I thought this promotion meant the world to you?"

"It did. It *does*," she corrected. "But the baby means more. I'll have some files sent over and can work from home. There's not that long before the second trimester starts and, if my blood pressure is better, I'll go back then."

Warm approval flared in his eyes. "And I'll be here at night."

Her heart missed a beat, both at his words and the casual way he delivered them. "What makes you think you'll be here?"

"Dr. Crosby told us to minimize your time alone. I'll sleep on the couch and be here while you shower. While

I'm at work, you can do safe things. Work on your cases at the table, watch television. Sleep."

"I won't be sleeping. I have a full caseload." She'd have Arthur bring files and notes over straight away and she could log on to the firm's email server from her laptop. Maybe it wouldn't need to be classed as time off. Just working from home.

"Sure, as long as they're things you can do sitting or lying down."

Was he questioning her commitment to the care of their baby? Her spine straightened. "Have no doubts, JT, I won't jeopardize this baby."

He arched a brow. "Then you won't have a problem with my sleeping on the couch in case you faint again."

Pia let out a breath. She'd been over and over this on the cab ride, too, and had to face that her options were fairly limited. She could stay with one of her sisters and her family, or she could stay with her parents. Both options involved moving back to her hometown of Pine Shores—too far from the office to have someone regularly drop off or pick up work.

Or she could accept this offer from her baby's father—a man who had as much to lose as she did if she fell and didn't have help. Why even hesitate? There would be minimal disruption to her work, and JT would simply be carrying out fatherly responsibilities. Of course, her work would have a problem with it if they found out, but it shouldn't be hard to conceal if she was careful.

She looked up at his darkly beautiful profile, into the depths of his dark-fringed eyes, at the small scar above his lip and her pulse began to jump madly.

She almost groaned. *This* was why she needed to be cautious. Could she resist the sublime lure of him if he slept five paces from her bed? If she rose in the night for a glass of water and saw his face relaxed in sleep, his limbs strewn across her couch? If he emerged from her bathroom with damp skin and her towel wrapped around his waist? How strong was her resistance exactly?

Yet, she *couldn't* start an affair with JT. Soon, she'd be a mother, and mothers needed to be sensible. Rational. Prudent. Around JT, she'd never been any of these things. She wasn't sure any of them were remotely possible when he was near.

And now that they would have an ongoing relationship through their baby, she'd need to be even more careful to keep things on an even keel, to ensure she and JT could sustain a lifelong connection. If they stepped too close to the fire again, could they walk away and remain on pleasant enough terms to share the parenting of their child? The last time they broke up, she'd had to sever things completely. That wouldn't be an option when they shared custody.

But—her hands crept to her belly—her weakness wasn't the issue. Her baby needed her to accept the help on offer. Her baby was depending on her to put every possible safety net in place to keep her or him protected.

She swallowed past the resistance in her throat and met his gaze. "You can stay."

Seven

Dusk was falling when JT came back. Pia had asked her assistant to bring over her briefcase and laptop—which she'd left on her desk when she'd ducked out for her ill-fated lunch break—plus the case files she was working on…except the Bramson estate.

Linda Adams had appointments all afternoon and Pia hadn't had a chance to talk to her yet, but now the will was Linda's responsibility, Pia needed to know how she wanted her to work on it from home. Ethically, she couldn't have paperwork pertaining to the case in the same apartment where a claimant was staying and could stumble across it, so she'd have to find a solution.

Unfortunately, Arthur hadn't arrived with her things yet—he'd needed to cover for her in a couple of meetings and said he'd drop them off in the morning.

Home alone with nothing to do, the anxieties raised by the day couldn't be pushed aside and they preyed on her mind… What if she lost this baby, too? A clammy shiver raced across her skin. If that happened, then she wouldn't survive either.

And JT staying here? How would she keep up her guard with him on her couch? He was dangerous for her, she'd known that—he brought out the worst in her. With him at her side, she'd always succumbed to reckless abandon, doing things against her own best interests. Within four weeks of his swaggering back into her life, she'd compromised herself at work, fallen pregnant and now had him sleeping in her apartment.

As her brain worked overtime, her fingers had itched for something to do, a contract to read, anything. So, under the gaze of an ever-watchful Winston, she'd found herself pulling out the bags she kept tucked away at the bottom of her wardrobe, and spreading her hat-making materials over the dining table. When JT arrived, she was working on a series of elaborate bronze petals that needed so much concentration that she almost managed to silence her fears.

He walked in with a sports bag, a suit hanger and an expression of determined cheerfulness. Even with the grimly false expression, his face had such masculine beauty that it stole her breath—the full bottom lip, the shadowed jaw, the brown waves falling across his forehead.

"How are you feeling?" he asked. No greeting, no pleasantries.

"I'm fine," she said, closing the door behind him and scowling. Partly about her reaction to him, but also because of his way of handling the situation. She might be worried about the baby, but JT regularly checking on her would only make her more anxious. "If you're going to stay here—"

"I am."

"—then I don't want you hovering and asking me how I feel all the time."

The corners of his mouth twitched, but he resisted the grin that lurked. "How would you like me to ascertain your condition?"

She stepped back. "I'll tell you if there's something wrong."

"Another ground rule, Pia?" he drawled, eyes lazily resting on her lips.

Her thoughts strayed to the last time they'd discussed ground rules…and the heated kiss that had followed. Goose bumps erupted across her skin. Dare she start them down that path once more? She folded her arms under her breasts. Things were different now. Neither of them would be that irresponsible or rash again. Would they?

"Yes, it's a ground rule," she said, lifting her chin.

He folded his arms over his muscled chest, mirroring her pose. "Then I get to add another one. I won't ask you how you feel, but you'll accept the things I do for the health of the woman who's carrying my baby."

Their gazes locked for timeless moments in a mini battle of wills until she looked away and sighed. He had as much investment in this pregnancy as she did. He might seem devil-may-care to the rest of the world, but she'd known him when they were teenagers, had seen how excited he'd been about becoming a father. The memory still brought searing tears to her eyes. And she'd witnessed his raw grief only weeks ago when he'd shown her the cross he'd carved.

Her health *was* the baby's health for now, so how could she deny his request?

"As long as it's within reason," she conceded.

"I'm always reasonable, princess." He dropped his bag beside the couch, his burgundy tie falling askew with the movement. He held up his suit bag. "Is there somewhere I can hang this?"

She considered suggesting the coat stand beside the door because he'd called her princess again, but that would be unfairly bad-mannered. Now—when she needed to keep distance—was not the time to lose her manners or composure.

She reached for the bag. "I'll hang it in my closet."

And so the blurring of boundaries begins, she thought. Although, to be honest, that had started when he'd made love to her under the stars. No, when he'd appeared from her firm's elevator and started a chain reaction of events, each more disastrous for her than the last.

"I appreciate it," he said as she walked into her room and hung his clothes among hers. When she came back he was leaning a hip against the dining room table, fingers sampling the texture of a roll of pale cream netting.

He looked up and smiled his crooked smile. "This reminds me of the fabrics and ribbons you used to have strewn across your bedroom."

A vision of a younger, leaner JT taunted her, of him climbing through her bedroom window and kissing her senseless. Her breaths began to come faster even as she tried to regulate them, and she frowned. Had he mentioned the past on purpose? It seemed he was always throwing her off balance by reminding her of the girl she'd once been, and the boy she'd known then. It was hard enough to deal with the present circumstances without his constant reminders of their past.

She picked up the netting, rerolled it into a tight ball, and spoke over her shoulder. "I'm not that girl, you're not that boy, you're not climbing into my bedroom and this is nothing more than a purely practical hobby."

"That's right," he said pokerfaced. "It's purely practical."

"They're expensive to buy and I have a difficult head shape to fit. I only make what I need." Yet today—for the first time—she'd started a hat she *didn't* need, and that made her uneasy. She chewed on one side of her bottom lip.

He opened his mouth to reply, but he met her eyes for a long moment, then closed it again before turning away. "I'll start on dinner if you want to take a shower or something else you need to do while I'm in the apartment."

She hesitated, bag of millinery supplies in her hand, and watched him drop his jacket on the back of a chair and walk into her kitchen with long strides. "You don't have to make dinner," she said. "There's no health risk in my cooking."

He shrugged as he opened a cupboard and scanned the contents. "How about we say I'm cooking myself dinner and making extra to share with you."

She sighed. They were having meals together now. Merrily sharing chores. Long past the concept of blurred boundaries. She hugged the bag of ribbons, velvet and elastic to her chest. While her heart struggled with the changes, her practical side warned not to look a gift horse in the mouth.

"Thank you," she said, dropping the bag back on the table and headed for the shower.

It was going to be a long couple of months until her second trimester.

A week later, JT threw down his pen, yawned and stretched at his desk—sleeping on Pia's couch was a killer on his spine. He had a pile of work in his in-tray, but all he could think about was Pia at home, driving herself crazy with boredom. She'd been doing menial work that other lawyers in the office were sending home on Arthur's daily courier visits, which obviously wasn't enough to keep her mind off her anxiety about the pregnancy.

Worse, Dr. Crosby had said Pia's stress would adversely affect the baby. He'd done some research on the web since then that had confirmed it—he needed Pia to be as relaxed as possible. The only times he'd seen her anywhere near being relaxed was when she created things with ribbon, wire and fabric. She got into a rhythm and her shoulders lost some of their tension.

He glanced across at his diary. The only appointments he had for the rest of the day were with people who worked for him—easy enough to reschedule. He picked up his briefcase and strode out to his personal assistant's desk.

"Mandy, clear my calendar for the rest of the day."

Displaying the efficiency and calmness he'd hired her for, she didn't bat an eyelash. "Certainly, Mr. Hartley. Will you be back?"

"Not this afternoon." He hit the elevator's down arrow. "You'll be able to reach me on my cell if you need to."

Once he was in the basement garage, he pulled out his phone and checked for the location of the closest millinery supplies shop, and by the time he reached Pia's apartment, he had three bags of assorted products.

He buzzed the intercom and waited for her to release the lock to the outside door. He'd suggested she give him a key, but she'd been less than enthusiastic—citing reasons like the short length of his stay.

Truth was, she was keeping him at arm's length and that wasn't a bad strategy given that every moment he was in her apartment he wanted to take her in his arms and back her over to that bed in her room. Or the table. Or the wall. Most times, he wasn't fussy. He simply wanted her with an intensity that was difficult to hide.

But he *had* pretty much kept it under wraps for the same

reason she'd refused him a key—he wasn't prepared to be lulled into any false states of security, and letting down his guard.

When Pia opened the apartment door, her gaze dropped to the bags. Her hair fell in waves about her shoulders and as she tucked some behind her ears, the elegant, pale skin of her cheek was exposed. A slow burn began down low.

He cleared his throat and handed one of the bags over. "I thought you could use these."

As she opened the handles, her eyes flicked to his, wide with surprise. "You didn't have to do this."

Dragging his gaze from the radiance in her eyes, he shrugged and handed her the other bags. "You're stuck here all day. I thought it might help."

Her violet eyes glistened. "That was thoughtful. Thank you." She peeped into the second bag. "You came home early just for this?"

"Pretty much." He walked in and slipped his arms from his jacket.

At one end of the dining table Pia had legal documents in piles and at the other end was a pea green creation with a wide brim. Seemingly unable to help herself, she was drawing a roll of snowy white ribbon from the bag he'd brought and was holding it against the hat.

"The woman in the shop said it was a versatile ribbon," he offered. He'd been unsure how versatile ribbon could be, but he'd taken her word for it.

"It's double-faced satin. There are a few things I could do with it." She looped it around a few fingers and it became a flower which she held against the hat again, judging its effect. She'd always been able to do that—transform rudimentary materials into a work of art. Dresses, jewelry, shawls, whatever she tried.

Among her family of hard, dull stones, she'd been a

polished ruby, bright and dazzling. And the pull of that luminescence had been stronger than a siren's call for a hard-edged boy from the wrong side of the tracks.

"Why did you give up dreams of fashion design, Pia?" he asked, moving behind her.

She turned, her startled eyes meeting his, and he glimpsed endless depths of sadness. His chest constricted at being confronted by that bleakness in eyes he'd seen shine with passion and joy.

Then she blinked it away and methodically packed the ribbon into the bag it'd come in. "I grew up."

Something told him this was too important to her, to them, to brush off. Perhaps it was her repeated use of that phrase. Perhaps it was the stark sadness he'd seen in her eyes. He sat on the edge of his couch bed, resting his loosely linked hands between his knees. "So you've said. What does that mean?"

She grew still, then laid the bag he'd given her on the table and sat on the edge of the couch with him. "I guess it's better you understand," she said, her voice tentative. "When I fell out that window and our baby..." Her voice trailed off and she swallowed. "I realized I had to stop acting like an indulged child. That included choosing a more sensible career and facing some hard truths about us."

Hard truths? Every muscle in his body clamped down, as if preparing for a blow. "That's when you broke up with me," he said without looking at her.

From the corner of his eye, he saw her flinch. "I had to, JT. Being with you brings out the worst parts of me. Every whim, every reckless impulse. And that's not a safe way to live. If we'd stayed together we would have self-destructed. It was too much. *We* were too much together. Surely you can see that now looking back?"

His mouth opened to reply, but words failed him. He'd be damned if he'd lie to make her feel better about her actions. The only self-destruction that would have happened was from her doing a cut and run later rather than sooner. If she'd had the courage to stand with him, to simply *stay*, they could have achieved anything together. So, no, he *couldn't* see that they'd been "too much together" when he looked back.

But what he *could* finally see was how she'd justified her actions for all these years. He shook his head. "You've been with *safe* men in the intervening years, I gather?"

Her eyes darted to his, then away again. "They were men who brought out the best in me."

He snorted. "None of them lasted, I see."

"Neither did we," she said, raising one eyebrow.

"Because you broke it off." *As soon as the going got tough.* He gritted his teeth.

"My recklessness killed our baby, JT. I won't let anything happen to this baby, and that means us keeping our emotional distance. I'll be a better mother this way. The mother our baby deserves."

His veins filled with ice. They might have different perspectives on the past, but on this they could agree—her plan suited him just fine. The last thing he needed was Pia getting thoughts into her head about anything more than co-parenting. When they were young and had dreams of being a family, being together forever, he'd forgotten that nothing is permanent. And that was dangerous. Since then, he'd kept up the pattern from his early childhood of never settling anywhere, moving apartments regularly.

Never getting too comfortable, never thinking he had it made, was important to keep the edge in business. *Everything changes*—business and personal. It was a lesson the woman beside him reinforced when she abandoned him the day after their first baby died.

But regardless of how things stood between them, one thing was for sure: He was no Warner Bramson. He hoped to God he'd inherited nothing beyond hair color from that poor excuse of a man, especially his idea of being a father, which had included sending his lover for an abortion and then abandoning her.

He would stand by Pia and their child no matter what it took.

Pia watched JT digest her words, praying she hadn't been too harsh but knowing she needed all her cards on the table. No misunderstandings, no cross-purposes.

Then he looked up. "If the baby survives the second trimester, we'll get married," he said through a clenched jaw.

Emotion stung the back of her nose. He might be bad for her, but JT Hartley was a good man. He was doing the right thing, even as it tore him up inside.

"JT, I'm not marrying you," she said gently but firmly. "I just explained why I can't."

"I'm not talking about hearts and flowers and illusions this time." His eyes were as hard as granite. "I'm talking about our baby having parents who are legally married."

Imagining that torturous scenario, she stifled a shudder. To be this close to the man who set her body alight, every day and night for the rest of her life, but not having him? "My answer is still no."

He nodded once, slowly, not meeting her eyes. "Okay, if the baby makes it to term, we'll discuss it again."

A shaft of afternoon sunlight fell across his face, glinting in his dark hair, illuminating the green of his eyes. She wanted to smile at the majesty of JT. Then, replaying what he'd said, the word "if" jumped out—he'd used it more than once…and understanding dawned. She might be worried about the baby and terrified she'd hurt the tiny person cradled in her womb, but JT didn't believe their baby would survive.

She laid a hand on his thigh, over the strong muscle that was as tense as the rest of him. "JT, you know this baby has a very good chance of making it, don't you? It won't be like the first time."

He looked at her with eyes that held a world of pain. He'd taken her to the cross he'd carved to help with her grief, but he'd never had a chance to grieve properly himself. Parents should be able to turn to each other at a time like that, but she'd had to break away for her own sanity.

"What did you do when Brianna died?" she asked softly.

He let out a humorless laugh. "Tried to get in to see you mostly."

The guilt of the pain she'd caused him stabbed into her chest like a hot knife. She swallowed once, twice, to make her voice work. "*After* that. After we spoke."

"Went a little wild, I suppose." He rubbed his chin and frowned. "When I left your hospital room, I got on my bike and rode till I ran out of gas. Then I filled up and rode some more."

A vision of him then, so young, so vulnerable, flashed in her mind. "JT, I'm so sorry," she said, her voice barely more than a rasp.

"You did me a favor. One thing I learned from growing up the way I did was that nothing's permanent," he said, his tone flat. Emotionless. "Nothing lasts. When we were together, I forgot that for a little while."

Her hand rose up to circle her throat. This man, who felt so familiar in some ways, was a complete stranger in others. "Do you really believe that?"

"Forever is a fairy tale told to kids." His lips thinned to a tight line. "Maturity is knowing it's false and *nothing's* forever."

She reached for his hand and laid it over her belly. "Not even this baby?"

His jaw clenched and he retracted his hand, obviously unwilling to share his dark fears any further. "We'll wait and see."

Her heart bled. The world had done this to him. His father, the people who wouldn't accept the new boy whenever he changed towns. And worst of all was knowing the part she'd played in creating this darkness inside him.

"JT, I hate that—"

"Princess," he cut her off, cynicism lacing his words, "the last thing I want or need is your sympathy."

Of course he wouldn't want her sympathy. She flinched. He wanted nothing from her anymore.

Except one thing.

There was one thing he wanted from her. And it was the only thing she could give him. After everything she'd robbed him of in the past—his child, their relationship, his belief in forever—she had to give him something in this moment. To take away the bleak loss from his eyes.

Heart in her mouth, she stood and gently pushed him back farther into the couch. He allowed the move, but watched her with wary eyes. Then she sank into his lap and rested her hands on his chest.

"What are you doing, Pia?" he asked wearily.

Truth be told, she wasn't exactly sure—it was the only plan that had come to mind. And now she was so close, enveloped by his scent, feeling his skin's heat through the fabric of his shirt, she didn't want to leave. Her pulse picked up, warming her skin, her body.

"We may not make a good couple—" she skimmed her

hands across his broad shoulders "—but there's something we do together that's magic."

"And that is?" he said, his voice forbidding, yet strained at the edges.

Nerves across her skin tingled in anticipation. She might have started this to bring the light back to his eyes, but JT filled every thought, every sense, until reasons blurred in her mind and she simply wanted.

Leaning down, her mouth a whisper from his, she said, "Kiss me, JT."

He didn't move, didn't bring his mouth closer, but his heart thumped hard under her hands and hers raced in a matching rhythm. Heaviness suffused her limbs and she wanted to melt into him.

"Why?" he asked, his features hardening.

His breath feathered over her face—coffee and pure JT—and her need beat louder. "Because we can," she whispered.

Eyes cold and remote, he picked her up and deposited her beside him on the couch. "I don't want pity sex, Pia."

Robbed of his warmth, of the intimacy of touch, she struggled to make her brain work. "You," she began weakly, then stopped. "You don't want me?"

Coughing out a humorless laugh, he stood and stalked to the other side of the room. "I'd have to be dead to not want you."

She blinked rapidly, focusing on JT's words over the sound of her still-racing heart. He wanted her but was rejecting her because he'd somehow picked up on what had been going on in her mind earlier. She may have been feeling sympathetic ten minutes ago, but that had morphed into something else the moment she'd touched him. Which always seemed to happen with this man.

"The way I feel in this moment isn't pity, I promise you," she said as she stood from her place on the sofa.

Long fingers speared through his hair as he gripped on to a handful of dark waves by the roots. "When you want me," he said, dropping his arm, his eyes intense, "purely for the sake of making love with me, then say the word. Tell me that and I'll be here."

For a whole week of having him in her apartment, she'd managed to keep her distance, to not walk to his makeshift bed in the middle of the night and crawl under the blankets with him. But that ended now. Her skin tightened unbearably. One more minute without him touching her was beyond endurance.

She followed and stood before him, heart thudding an uneven rhythm.

"JT, what's the word?" she asked quietly.

A muscle worked on the side of his jaw. "What do you mean?"

"The word I can say—" on shaking legs, she took a small step forward, to within touching distance "—if I want you. Just for the sake of making love with you."

His eyes half closed, masking his expression. "You want that word now?"

"You said you'd be here if I say it." She moistened her dry lips and he watched the motion. "I want to know what it is."

A battle raged inside him, she could feel it pulling him in two directions at once, his body held rigid as the war thundered on.

"My name," he finally said as if the words were ripped from his throat. "All you ever have to do is say my name and mean it."

"JT," she said and reached for his hand with trembling fingers. She could feel the beat of his heart in her blood.

As he interlaced his fingers with hers, his other hand tucked wayward strands of her hair behind her ears. "You really want this?"

Need for him clawed inside her, stole her breath, and she had to be honest. "I've been trying to deny it for fourteen years, but I've never wanted any other man the way I wanted—still want—you. Every moment of every day. With everything inside me."

A shiver ran through his body and his hands clenched into fists at his sides. "Pia, I can't promise—"

"I don't want promises. That route doesn't work for us, but *this*," she said as she brought his hand to her waist. "This," she said as she kissed the roughness of his chin. "This is something I want more than I can say."

He looked into her eyes for a long moment, then he lifted her chin with gentle fingers and his sensual lips touched hers.

Eight

Pia parted her lips as JT's mouth captured hers, needing his kiss more than she could ever imagine needing another thing on this earth. Heat bloomed under her skin as his lips moved slowly, deliciously across hers.

And with that one kiss, the fire between them exploded to life, blazing as hot as ever. This was the passion that had been missing in other relationships. Only JT had ever inspired anything close to this level of flammability. She bit gently at his bottom lip, sucking it into her mouth and he groaned low in his throat. The sound reverberated through her body, all the way down to a spot below her navel that pulled tight with need.

His arms encircled her waist, drawing her closer, and wanting *more,* she scraped her nails over the fabric covering his back, wanting *everything.* There was something wild and wanton about making love with JT. His teeth scraped at the hollow of her shoulder and a jolt of searing pleasure washed through her. With other lovers, it'd been more like sex-by-numbers, pleasurable but predictable. With JT, it was as if anything were possible—exhilarating, but a little scary for the tenuous thread she held on her self-control. Which was why she'd been wary of seeing him again—he brought out the bad side of her. The wanton, obsessive, *crazy* side of her. But—she stroked her thumbs along his biceps—the time for second-guessing and backtracking was gone. She needed him here and now. Any fallout could be dealt with later.

Fingers jittery, desperate, she pulled the tails of his shirt from his trousers and ran her hands up his chest. His skin was smooth and scorching and when she met the smattering of hair in the middle of his chest, she traced the pads of her fingers across it, reveling in the crisp sensation.

"There's no one in the world like you," he said close to her ear, his breath warm and fast, and she melted a little more. He kissed her again, tongue sliding in an erotic, wet caress inside her mouth and she closed her eyes, drunk on the dark male flavor of him. She couldn't bear to end the kiss, wanting to stay connected to him forever, until finally she broke away to drag air into her burning lungs.

He walked her backward, toward her bedroom door, and she let him guide her steps, pulling his tie loose on the way. The tie landed on the back of a chair and her fingers set to unbuttoning his shirt.

As she worked, his hands slid over the sides of her breasts and she shivered. Simple touches—all he had to do was *touch* her and she was his for the taking. All he'd ever had to do was touch her…

As his shirt fell on the floor, she tugged his belt loose and discarded it, and he walked her backward again until the backs of her legs met the side of her bed. With nowhere left to go, she was pinned to the edge of the high mattress as he pressed along her, the jut of his erection pushing against her belly. She swayed side to side—small, slow movements—to better feel the shape of him.

Eyes dark with need, he reached around to unzip her dress and pushed it down over her shoulders. The rush of cool air on her sensitized skin was like a caress. JT's eyes swept over her before he groaned and sank to his knees, pressing his head against her stomach, his arms wrapped tightly around her.

"JT," she whispered, threading her fingers through his thick hair, unable to verbalize everything she felt. No one but him had ever looked at her body as if it were a gift.

He pressed kisses to her abdomen, to her hip, to where the lacy panties met her leg, then he pulled the fabric aside and kissed the apex of her thighs. A delicious haze descended and her fingers in his hair pulled tight. The erotic motion of his tongue was almost too much to bear, but his broad palms held her in place. Her skin was too tight for her body, as if she was expanding, growing…

When he stood, she was vibrating with need. She unzipped his trousers and let them slide away before catching the sides of his deep blue boxers and pushing them down along the same path. She circled his bare erection with a hand and air hissed out from between his teeth. The hot-satin feel of him against her palm was everything she remembered. When they'd made love on the beach again, they'd moved too fast for her to appreciate the sensations like this, and she'd regretted it when she'd lain awake in the weeks afterward. This time, she was taking her time, gathering as many memories as she could.

He held her gaze, and as she caressed him with her fingertips she began to lose herself in the clear green depths of his eyes. Somewhere inside her, the girl she'd once been was clawing her way to the surface, responding to the younger JT who still lurked in those eyes. Her JT. She stilled and whispered, "I've missed you."

His eyes drifted closed for a long moment and he squeezed them tight, his entire face clenching, growing hard. When he opened them again, any trace of the boy was gone, and he was pure man, filled with nothing but desire. He grabbed both her hands, turning her so he could sink down onto the bed, gently pulling her on top of him. The feel of his body pressed against hers, the slide of their skin was nirvana itself. He grasped her bottom and positioned her to increase the friction, and she shimmied up a little to help, her breaths coming faster. Their bodies matched each other, as if his had been created to lie alongside hers, and together they became more than they could ever be apart.

With near-frenzied need, her hands stroked over his skin, touching everywhere she could reach, and in a synchronized rhythm, his hands moved in a similar pattern, caressing her sides, her hips, her back. His hands had more roughness than a businessman's should, and the sensation pushed her closer to the edge.

Smoothly, he rolled her over and hovered in the air, hands resting near her shoulders. The absence of his touch was almost painful. "Come back to me," she urged, grasping at him.

A slow, devilish smile spread across his face and he leaned down to kiss her hungrily, harder, deeper. The fire inside erupted into a roaring bonfire, the flames threatening to consume her as she grasped at him, pulling him to her, as he positioned himself between her knees. When he entered her, it was with a thrust too gentle. She arched beneath him, urging, wanting, needing. Heeding her call, or perhaps the demands of his own body, he moved faster, harder and she gripped his shoulders and moved with him.

The hedonistic pleasure of the slick slide of their bodies was the beginning of the end, the pressure building down deep inside, until he tipped them both over the edge in a release more intense, more explosive than anything they'd shared before, leaving her gasping for air, her limbs helplessly slumped back on the bedcovers. JT slid to the side to lay in her arms, pressed against her, his breathing labored, not moving any other muscles than those needed to fill his lungs.

She glanced over at him, and a secret smile filled her chest as she took in his sensual form sprawled across her bed. She'd never invited a man into her own bed before, even when she'd been engaged—it was something far too intimate—but JT was different. He'd always been different. Despite their having no future as a couple, at this moment he somehow belonged in her bed. She snuggled into his solid warmth.

As her body began to return to some sense of normality and the air turned cold on her skin, JT pulled her comforter from the end of the bed and wrapped it around them, gathering her close beneath it. She sighed and laid her head on his chest.

"Pia," he said, his voice rumbling beneath her cheek, "about what I said before. No promises—"

She turned and laid a finger over his lips. "I don't need them, JT. Neither of us wants to go there again."

He stretched and tucked the arm that wasn't holding her behind his head. "The problem with that is you're pregnant."

A powerful mix of apprehension and excitement filled her chest at his reminder of the tiny life in her womb. But she knew that wasn't what would be going through JT's mind. It'd be all about doing the right thing. Responsibilities and obligations.

"Actually, there's one promise you need to make me," she said, lifting herself to lean on an elbow and looking down at him.

His eyes were immediately wary. "What's that?"

"I don't want you doing the 'right thing' or what you think the right thing is. If we're going to get through this, we need to be honest with each other." She stroked a finger down his cheek. "You don't want to marry me, JT, so please don't ask again."

There was a long minute of silence, when the only sounds she could hear were the cars on her street and JT's still-heavy breathing. She bit down on the side of her lip and waited. They couldn't waste their energy arguing over details when they needed to be on the same side.

Then he nodded. "I'll see what I can do," he said and pulled her against him again, tucking her head into the curve of his shoulder. She relaxed into the embrace, glad they were at least on the same page about marriage.

Her cell rang and she groped for her handbag beside the bed and fumbled for the phone. Ryder Bramson's name appeared on the screen. She flinched but years of conditioning meant she could never let a client's call go. "I have to take this," she said to JT. "It's work."

He reached for a magazine from a bedside table, obviously planning to give her some privacy. It wouldn't be enough, but it would be something—she would just need to be careful with what she said.

Straightening her shoulders and slipping into professional mode, she clicked the talk button. "Hello, Mr. Bramson."

She felt JT stiffen beside her and heard the magazine

being dropped back on the table as he moved up to sit against the headboard.

Ryder Bramson's deep, commanding voice came down the line. "Good afternoon, Ms. Baxter. I've had a call from a woman named Linda Adams who tells me she's taken the lead on administering my father's estate."

Her heart bumped around in her chest as she swung her legs over the side of the bed and stood. "That's true."

"Why the change? I was happy with you."

She lifted a hand to circle her throat. This wouldn't be an easy conversation to have in front of JT and not give anything away, but her apartment was small enough that wherever she went, he'd overhear. She could tell Ryder that it was a bad time and ring him when JT wasn't around, but when would that be? Tomorrow? Ryder Bramson would want answers before then. Running out of options, she crossed the room and leaned against the window frame. If anything confidential came up, she'd refer him back to Linda Adams.

"I'm sorry, Mr. Bramson," she said, using a calm, controlled voice, "but it's no longer possible for me to head up that case."

"I'd like to know why," he repeated.

Pressing a hand to her temple, she gripped the phone tightly. How much could she reasonably say with JT in the room? She concentrated, trying to get her post-lovemaking brain to function, and knew the answer—the information his lawyer could find by ringing her firm.

Glad to have a line in the sand for the phone call, she expelled a breath. "A conflict of interest has arisen and it's better that I step back. Linda has taken the lead and I'm assisting her."

"A conflict of interest? Tell me," Ryder said, voice suddenly like steel.

Her heart stuttered like a jackhammer. "It would be better—"

"Pia, we've been working with you for some time on this, and been happy with your work. But if you have a conflict of interest, then I think I deserve to know what that is." His voice lightened. "You've found you're another of Warner's long-lost children?"

She glanced at JT, sitting up against the headboard, hair rumpled, comforter strewn around his thighs, not even pretending to not listen in. Despite the seriousness of the phone call, a quivering began down low in her belly.

"No," she said slowly, turning away, "but I have an unacceptable link to someone who claims to be one of those children."

There was a sharply inhaled breath down the line. "You've met Hartley?"

She looked back at the gloriously naked man in her bed. "Yes."

"To have handed over the case, it must be serious. You're somehow involved, I take it?"

Involved? Try pregnant with the man's child. "You could say that," she said, trying not to let the irony come through in her voice.

"Then I can see why you need to step back." He sighed with what sounded like disappointment.

She squeezed her eyes shut, hating that she'd let everyone down—the firm, Ryder Bramson, herself. It reminded her too much of her childhood where she was constantly facing her parents' disappointment.

Then she made herself put it all behind her and stood taller against the bedroom wall. All she could do from here was ensure she didn't make one more mistake—even a spelling mistake, as Ted Howard had helpfully pointed out—and to reassure Ryder that things weren't as bad as he might be imagining, for the firm's sake as well as hers.

"I promise you, Mr. Bramson," she said, injecting her words with confidence, "the firm's integrity has never been, nor will it be, compromised. As soon as I realized I couldn't work with the necessary detachment, I excused myself from the case."

There was silence for a moment before he let out a breath. "I appreciate that. Tell me something, off the record. Since you've come to know him, do you personally believe his claim to be Warner's son?"

She looked at JT while she had his half brother on the phone, acutely aware she was trapped between two powerful men. All she could do was tell the truth. "Yes, I believe him. But that won't affect the way I carry out my duties assisting Linda Adams."

"Okay, good to know. Thanks for your work on the case and your honesty."

She thumbed the off button and dropped the cell on her bedside table, moving slowly to give herself the extra few moments to compose herself before facing JT. She pulled a white silky robe from her cupboard and slipped her arms through the sleeves, then sat on the side of the bed.

"That was one of Warner's sons," she said needlessly as she looked at him.

His eyes were shuttered against her, his arms folded over his bare chest. "Can you tell me which one, or is that privileged information?"

"Ryder." Being in the room with her during that call was probably as close as he'd ever come to either of his half brothers—to anyone on the paternal side of his family—so she waited patiently for him to process the information.

JT nodded. "The legitimate one."

"Yes," she said, wishing she could climb back into the

bed and hold him, to find what he needed in this moment and give it to him. But JT Hartley wasn't a man who appreciated any form of sympathy. Especially from her. He'd shared his body, but he hadn't shared even a sliver of his heart.

"Apparently," he said, the bitterness only faint in his voice, "it was to protect Warner's engagement to Ryder's mother that my mother was chased out of town."

"Warner's wife came from a rich family." She didn't like to be cynical, but the media had speculated for years that the reason Warner hadn't divorced his wife and married his long-term mistress was the chance he'd lose too much money in the process—most of the money had come from her. A man like that wouldn't want his financially advantageous marriage jeopardized before it had started.

He cocked his head to the side. "What do you think of Ryder?"

She thought of the tall man with the rugged features. He was straight down the line and had been nothing but courteous to her. "I think he's a good man."

"A good man who married to get more stock in his family company." He arched an eyebrow. "That sounds a whole lot like his father to me."

The media had gone crazy when Ryder's engagement to Macy Ashley had been leaked, and the implications for Bramson Holdings became apparent—he acquired her family company and its ten-percent stock in Bramson Holdings at their wedding. Perfect timing as he headed into a battle for control of the board with his other half brother, Seth Kentrell.

"I know it appeared that way, but I've seen Ryder with Macy and there's something special between them. They're in love." Pia's insides had twisted tight when she met Macy at a fundraising ball and seen her obvious affection for her husband, and his for her.

JT's eyes said he didn't believe it, but he didn't say the words aloud. "Have you met the other one?"

She nodded. "Seth Kentrell." Dark hair, midnight blue eyes, always in perfect control of himself and situations around him.

"Seems he's recently engaged, too," JT said with cynicism. "Again it had something to do with the family business."

"Not in the way you think. He had some delicate negotiations with April Fairchild over the ownership of a hotel. It would have been difficult for him, so soon after losing Jesse." Seth's brother—JT's third half brother—who'd recently died in a car accident. Her heart cramped as she remembered being the one to break the news to Ryder about a brother he'd never met. Such a sad, senseless loss of life.

"What was Jesse like?"

"Sweet." She climbed farther onto the bed and rested against the headboard within touching distance of JT. "He didn't seem to want anything to do with the family business."

"We had that in common," he said harshly. And she knew behind the harshness were seven levels of pain that he would always hide and that thought made tears threaten at the back of her eyes.

Knowing all the brothers, she could see the perspective of each. She'd give almost anything for Ryder and Seth to just acknowledge JT—or at least allow the DNA test that would prove the connection, then acknowledge him—but it was hard to judge their choices without having walked in their shoes.

She tucked her feet up under herself and pulled the

sash of her robe tighter. "Ryder and Seth are both good men stuck in an awkward position by their father. Under different circumstances, you'd probably like them both."

JT looked across at the woman he'd just made love to. A woman who seemed like a stranger in this moment. "You think I could like two men who actively work to keep their own biological brother from what should rightfully be his? To deny that he's even their brother?" He shook his head. "These don't sound like *good men* to me."

Restless, he stood and reached for his trousers. As he zipped them up, he ran back over the conversation she'd had with Ryder Bramson and his hands gradually stilled.

"You've been taken off the Bramson estate," he said without looking up. "Because of me."

She climbed out of the bed and began to collect her clothes from the floor. "Not removed completely, simply moved to assisting another lawyer who's taken the lead."

His gut clenched like a vise. Maybe he should have kept his distance. Her career could suffer because he'd involved her in his life again. Seemed he caused trouble for her no matter which decade they met in.

He rested his hands low on his hips. "They know you're pregnant and I'm the father."

She nodded as she slipped into her dress. "I told my boss the morning after we saw the doctor. I couldn't keep something like that from him. It would have been unethical."

She reached behind herself to do up her dress, but before she could find the zipper, he was there and pulled it up, holding her hair away from the teeth. "And he gave the case to someone else."

"I handed it over," she said as she turned around, tucking her hair behind her ears. "It was the right thing to do, if maybe a little later than I should have."

He remembered when they'd first discussed this, the night he'd come to her apartment on his bike, full of confidence and wanting to lay ghosts to rest.

"You badly want this case, don't you?"

"More than any other I've handled."

He narrowed his eyes. "You said you'd be up for a promotion if you handled the case well."

Her mouth twisted in a bad impersonation of a smile. "Turns out, becoming pregnant by a claimant to the will isn't anyone's idea of handling the case well."

Wincing, he let loose an oath. "I'm sorry, Pia."

"Don't sweat it." She shrugged and walked through to the living room. "He said that if I didn't make any more mistakes and handled the rest of my caseload flawlessly, I'd still be in the running."

Following her out, he rested a hip on the kitchen counter. "He must think highly of you." She shrugged self-effacingly, and his brain raced ahead. "Working from home during your first trimester, is that something that would put you out of the running?"

"He wouldn't say so officially," she said slowly, as she collected the bags of supplies he'd bought her, "but maybe. I've become less reliable to the firm in the last couple of months."

"Since I showed up," he said and blew out a breath, wishing he could kick himself.

She didn't answer. She didn't have to.

He'd compromised her career and there was no denying it. In fact, the paperwork for his claim on Warner Bramson's will was prepared and ready to be lodged, and that would cause things to heat up even more for her at work.

His eyes dropped to her belly, where their little boy or girl was safely nestled, and felt a twinge deep in his chest. They were in too far for him to walk away, but this wasn't fair for her. She'd told him to stay away the day he'd ambushed her at her office and he hadn't listened.

The one thing he *could* do for her was hold off on lodging the claim. He'd call his attorney, Hendricks, and tell him to put it in a drawer until Pia was back at work and able to fend for herself with her bosses. It was the least he should do.

Nine

As JT took her hand in his and they stepped out onto the bustling street from the downtown car park, Pia allowed herself to relax. Less than an hour ago, Dr. Crosby had given the all clear for Pia to return to work—now that her blood pressure was back in the normal range and she was into her second trimester. JT had suggested going out to dinner to celebrate. After being cooped up for so long, the idea had appealed. And because it had been an early evening appointment, they'd driven straight over to an Italian restaurant JT knew for an early meal.

Dusk was falling, the streetlights were casting shadows across the pavement, her baby was fine, and JT's hand was warm encircling hers—her heart sighed with the perfection of the moment.

She smiled up at him. "Thank you for suggesting this."

"You're welcome." His expression turned thoughtful as he guided her through a well-lit doorway into a brightly decorated but cozy restaurant. "I hadn't thought about you wanting to get out—I should have done it sooner."

A flamboyant waiter seated them and took their drinks orders, leaving them with menus. There were only two other tables occupied, but it was still too early for the dinner rush.

"The risotto is good here," JT said as he perused the list.

Unobserved, she looked at him over the top of her fold-out menu, at where the strong column of his throat met the crisp white collar of his shirt, at his sensual bottom lip, at the dark hair that fell over his forehead as he looked down. A delicious shiver raced across her skin. Risotto wasn't the only good thing here.

"Thanks for the tip," she said a little unevenly, "but I'm dying for a big bowl of pasta."

He glanced up, vibrant green eyes trained on her face. "You should have said. I can make pasta."

She shrugged and broke the eye contact. "The craving only started when you chose Italian."

The waiter arrived back with a flourish and took their order. Once they were alone, Pia looked out to the darkening street, brightness streaming down from streetlamps and from the headlights of passing cars. Two spindly trees on the sidewalk were covered in fairy lights that matched those on the front of the restaurant, creating a magical atmosphere. Her skin tingled. Anything seemed possible on this night that she and JT were joined in celebrating.

Since she'd invited him into her bed, he'd stayed, spending each night making glorious love to her. There had been no point playing coy and banishing him after she'd given her body to him once more. And in some ways, it had been inevitable that he'd ended up in her bed after he'd moved in—seeing him emerge from her bathroom in the mornings, chest bare, hair damp, had kept her on the very edge of temptation.

But it was for a short time, no routines, no dependence. That was what they'd agreed on.

Now that the doctor had given her a clean bill of health, indicating that her fainting risk was no higher than for any other pregnant woman, JT would be leaving again—they'd return to simply being parents of an unborn child. And if her chest hollowed a little at the thought, then it was lucky they weren't continuing the arrangement any longer than they had. Their bond was via their baby.

She reached for her bag and found a folded piece of note paper. "I've been thinking about names." She'd thumbed through the baby name book they'd used to choose Brianna's name yesterday while JT was at work. "I made a few notes as a starting point. Some for a boy and some for a girl."

Within an instant, his face hardened, a sharp contrast to the relaxed charm of only a minute ago. "It's too soon for names."

Her heart stuttered and dipped. He'd said he didn't want to plan too far ahead in case something happened to the baby, but she'd hoped that after today's clearance from the doctor, he'd be willing to look a little further into the future. To have some optimism about their baby.

"Dr. Crosby said everything looked fine," she said, finding a smile with effort. "And I'm into the second trimester now."

The waiter swooped past, depositing two glasses of sparkling water on their table. JT sipped from his, gripping it in a white-knuckled hold. "You were into the second trimester last time."

"I fell out a window last time," she pointed out. "I don't

plan on scaling any buildings, falling from any trees or climbing out any windows in the next few months."

He didn't even crack a smile at her attempt at humor. "Dr. Crosby said there was a ten-percent chance of a placental abruption reoccurring. I just don't want us to put the cart before the horse."

That figure of ten percent had haunted her dreams, but she refused to let the ice-cold fear crawl into her waking hours. Positivity was the only option—this baby would survive and be born healthy. And if JT accepted that too, it would be easier for her to keep the fears at bay.

"We haven't bought a crib," she began, speaking slowly, gently, "haven't decorated a nursery. I understand you want to play it safe and wait before doing big things, but there's nothing to lose in choosing some options for names."

The skin across his face pulled taut. "There's something to lose," he said and the pain in his eyes tore at her soul.

Opening their hearts to a new baby after such grief wasn't something covered in the baby books, but they had to find a way through it, for their child's sake.

Her hand strayed to her belly. "JT, things are going to constantly crop up from here on that will involve thinking about the future. How do you want to handle that?"

"One day at a time," he said in a tone that ended the discussion.

Their meals arrived and she watched him pick up his cutlery, his body still tense. The restaurant was slowly filling up but there was no one at the tables adjacent to theirs, so they had a modicum of privacy. She picked at her fettuccine—only minutes before she'd been craving this meal but now, instead of tasting the flavors, she could only think about JT's grief and inability to believe in this baby. They talked about the weather and topics that didn't hit any buttons—with Pia using a tone of artificial brightness to try and lift the mood—and when they finished, JT ordered them both another drink and finally the atmosphere at the table relaxed again.

"You were right about the food here," she said. "The pasta was delicious. How did you find this place?"

"I own the building," he said simply and reached for his glass.

His answer was so unexpected that she couldn't prevent a short laugh from escaping. "Of course you do."

He grinned crookedly back at her and more of the tension from earlier dissipated. "I haven't been here in a year, maybe two, and I was hoping the meals were as good as I remembered."

She sat back in her chair, wondering at his life. The restaurant wasn't that far from his office or apartment, and he liked the food. And yet he hadn't been for a year or two. Curious.

She fingered the edge of the red napkin. "Why don't you come more often?"

"I don't know." Frowning, he glanced from the brightly painted walls to the Italian flag behind the counter, as if he hadn't considered the question before. Then he shrugged his broad shoulders. "I never seem to get a chance. I work until late and if I don't want to cook for myself, I order in."

"You don't bring dates here?" she asked, then held her breath, wondering if she'd pressed too far into his personal life. But he didn't seem bothered.

"I don't date much. And when I do, I prefer something bigger and flashier." He meant to imply he was a big spender for his dates, it was in the glint in his eyes, but she didn't believe it. He was avoiding the intimacy a small place like this would bring.

He'd always been something of a lone wolf—which had

been part of his appeal to her sixteen-year-old self—and it seemed he was even more so now.

"You don't let women get close, do you, JT?"

For a split second, his eyes flashed fire, then it was gone. "I prefer to keep women and dates uncomplicated."

She'd seen into his soul in that split second. The raw pain that still lived there, the blame he held. That she deserved. She swallowed and faced the consequences of her actions. "Uncomplicated, meaning not letting anyone close enough to hurt you the way I did."

He stared at her with a fervent intensity for a long moment before lifting his glass and looking around the restaurant again.

"I'm sorry, JT," she whispered.

He flinched but didn't look back at her, his gaze fixed out the window, on the street's passing traffic. "Nothing to be sorry for." His voice was light. Too light. "You ended it early enough to save us both a lot of pain. Much better you did it when we were kids than a few years down the track when our lives were too integrated."

"I'm still sorry. I was so engulfed in my own grief that I handled everything badly. I should have explained more. Or something."

"I'll buy some pasta tomorrow," he said, blatantly changing the subject. "Now you have a craving for it, I'll make you some during the week."

Her heart flipped over in her chest. He was planning to stay? The only reason she'd let her guard down and allowed him to share her bed was they'd understood it was time-limited. A very short time frame. If he stayed longer, she wasn't sure if her defenses would last, and then she'd be back in the middle of loving him again. Unthinkable. Besides, she'd kept him from his own life for too long while he played nursemaid.

She ran a finger around the rim of her glass. "You were only staying for the first trimester. I'm over the danger now. You're free to leave."

"It would be safer if I stay."

"It would be safer if I admitted myself to hospital and was under constant surveillance from a medical team, but that would be overkill. I'll be fine on my own. I want to do this on my own."

His eyes narrowed, their green becoming darker, more intense. "I can't approve that plan."

"I promise I'll let you know if I have any problems, but I think you need to move back to your own place, don't you? We need to get things working…I don't know…working the way we're going to be working in the future."

He rubbed his hand over his shadowed chin, considering, and she wondered if he'd insist. And how could she possibly counter JT when he insisted?

He sipped his drink and watched her over the rim, his eyes heating. "I'd miss your bed too much to leave just yet."

Her skin prickled with awareness; her blood heated. She would miss him in her bed, too. The ache of his absence was already beginning to bloom throughout her body. But that was even more reason to make the break now—she couldn't fall into a false relationship with him, something based on sex and their shared baby. Lines had been too blurred, but going forward, they needed to be as clear as possible to protect everyone.

"We knew that your living with me would be temporary. And I appreciated your putting yourself out by staying with me."

"It's no hardship," he said, his eyes heavy-lidded.

Her heart skipped a beat. The pull of him was as powerful as ever and she had to call on all her reserves of strength not to snake her hand across the table just to feel his skin. They were playing with fire—why was she the only one to recognize that?

She arched an eyebrow and pinned him with a look. "Tell me, JT, do you want to be in a relationship with me? A future with all the trimmings? Vows and promises?"

A grimace passed across his face, as if he'd eaten something distasteful.

"No." The word was said softly, but with conviction and despite it being the answer she'd expected, the rejection nonetheless stung deep inside.

She stuffed the reaction away from her awareness and met his gaze. "Then don't let us fall into a relationship by default. If you stay, sleeping in my bed, preparing for our baby, we'll end up playing happy families and you'll be stuck in a simulated marriage without ever having chosen it."

His eyes widened as he took in her meaning, and seemed to finally understand how thin the ice they were skating on had become.

"I'll be gone tomorrow," he said, and called for their bill.

She watched him settle the account and then pull the chair out for her. He guided her from the restaurant, holding himself more distant than he had only minutes before. Her chest twisted as she acknowledged something between them had changed forever.

The next morning, JT was sliding scrambled eggs onto plates when Pia came into the kitchen tying a scarf around her neck. He paused and watched her make the loose knot. She was wearing the same cappuccino skirt and button-down jacket that she'd worn the day he'd first seen her again in her office. But this time she had a soft scarf in emerald and jade greens, her flame-bright hair falling about her shoulders instead of pinned back, and—his gaze dipped—open-toed shoes that exposed rose pink toenails. His pulse spiked. He'd always had a thing for painted toenails. But Pia had been right last night—he needed to keep his emotional distance and not fall into the trap of forming a faux relationship.

Co-parenting was one thing. But he would never again entrust his heart to her unreliable hands.

"Nice scarf," he said, pulling his gaze away and reaching for the pan of fried mushrooms.

She fingered the fabric. "Is it too much? I had some silk left after I made the trim on a straw hat the other day and thought it would match this suit."

Seeing her reclaiming some of who she was made him feel a little lighter, despite the way things were between them. "It's perfect. Orange juice is on the table, and breakfast is coming."

"I'll miss your cooking," she said casually as she looked around the kitchen. "Is that baked tomatoes I smell?"

He hesitated. Perhaps he should stay longer? Ensure she was eating properly for their baby. His resolve of the night before began to waver. No, she wanted him to go, it was the right thing for him to do, and she was an adult, more than capable of preparing healthy food for herself. He took the tomatoes from the oven and slid them onto the plates before carrying them out and setting them on the table.

He picked up his cutlery. "Pia, there's something I need to tell you."

"Sounds ominous," she said, then took a sip of juice.

He speared a mushroom with his fork, then paused to meet her eyes as he delivered the news. "My attorney is lodging my claim on the Bramson estate today. I wanted to wait till you were back at work."

She drew in a breath and nodded. “Thanks for telling me. And for waiting. You’re counting on there being no evidence Warner knew about you?”

“Yes.” He was sure now that none existed. The arrogant man must have assumed that when he frightened his poor secretary, she’d gone ahead and obtained an abortion. Gut burning, he stabbed another mushroom.

But the good news was if Warner hadn’t known about his existence, then it gave JT the standing to challenge the will. His attorney couldn’t foresee any problems, and once there were court-ordered DNA tests on Warner’s other two sons, the judge would have no choice but to split the inheritance three ways. His mother would finally get the public acknowledgment and compensation she’d been denied for thirty-one years.

And it all started today.

As did his new life back at his own apartment. He looked around Pia’s sweet dining and living rooms with their curtains and pink window seat. It surprised him, but he’d miss this apartment. Not the couch—it’d given him far too many kinks and sleepless nights before he moved into Pia’s bed. But still, he’d started to almost feel at home here....

He stabbed a tomato with his fork, annoyed that he’d let himself start to relax into something that was temporary.

“Before I leave this morning,” he said, “I’ll throw my things in the car, but I want you to promise me you’ll call if you have the slightest need.”

“More rules between us, JT?” she asked with a curve of her voluptuous lips. “Though, I think you’ll be the one needing help.”

He thought of his large, cold bed and decided she was probably right. But he also knew that wasn’t what she was referring to. “Help with what?”

"The media were always interested in the Bramson family, but since Warner's death, they've been frenzied around Ryder and Seth. Even when Ryder was in Australia, the paparazzi found him."

He remembered seeing that photo of Ryder kissing his future wife—it had been grainy and slightly blurred, but it'd been splashed over the internet and papers within hours of when it was taken. And she was right, everyone in the country knew the members of Warner Bramson's family—from the business pages the gossip pages, and the front pages.

"And," she said, scooping some eggs onto her fork, "with Seth's engagement to a world-famous singer, the media value of the Bramson family has grown even more. They won't let you rest in peace once this story hits their radars."

Something soft touched his calf. He looked down and saw Winston curling around his legs and under the chair. Absently, he leaned down to rub the cat's head. "I'm sure they'll run stories about it, but no one knows me—I'm not a media magnet like those two."

"Even if you're not as famous now as Ryder and Seth, you're also not used to the media attention. They grew up with it."

The few small brushes he'd had with the media had made his skin crawl. There had been ribbon cuttings and announcements of his company's new developments, but he left them to his PR department. Having his image, his words, beamed into houses all over the country was beyond an invasion of his privacy.

He'd heard of cultures where they believed taking a photo of someone would steal part of their soul and he'd sympathized with the theory. The public's appetite for gossip and celebrity pictures was insatiable. That had to strip away at a person, and it was something he would have no part of.

He swallowed a mouthful of black coffee. "The lifelong media attention is one thing I don't envy Bramson's other sons."

Pia's fork dangled from her fingers as she regarded him. "Tell me something honestly. If you could go back and choose now, would you want the childhoods they had, even with all the money?"

Not regularly changing schools? Enticing. Having enough money for everything he needed? Damn attractive. But he wouldn't have learned how to rebuild a bike, wouldn't have become as self-sufficient. Wouldn't have met Pia; for all the heartache of their teenage romance, it'd given him some of his happiest memories.

"No, I wouldn't trade my childhood for theirs. For better or for worse, it made me who I am." He finished the last swig of his coffee and put the mug on the table. "But I do wish my mother had their mothers' life instead of working menial jobs, never having anything for herself so I had enough, always looking over her shoulder."

"Have you told her yet?" she asked, her violet eyes both nervous and curious at the same time. "About the baby?"

They'd discussed this only last night. It was only the second trimester—far too early to get carried away with announcements. "If we make it to term."

"I'm sorry. I forgot you don't believe this baby will make it." She said the words without judgment, perhaps even with a touch of compassion, but there was a hurt behind them.

"I wouldn't say I don't believe," he said carefully.

Her head tilted to the side. "What would you say, then?"

"How about, I don't want increased pressure on you. No unnecessary scrutiny." Dr. Crosby had told them to watch

Pia's stress, and his mother's well-meaning excitement and eagerness to be involved was an extra pressure Pia didn't need right now. They needed to keep it simple. "That's why you still haven't told your parents yet, isn't it?"

"How do you know I haven't told them?" she asked, gaze on her plate.

He almost smiled. She needed to ask? The first clue was her father hadn't knocked on the door to warn him off. Her parents weren't the live-and-let-live kind. "Have you?"

"No," she admitted.

He was glad. Keep it simple. Low pressure. For Pia's health. "I understand why you needed to tell your boss." She had her ethics and that was a good thing. "But I want an agreement between us not to tell anyone else."

He looked into her clear, violet eyes and had to be brutally honest, if only with himself. Telling people, having conversations about their baby with someone other than their doctor, would make it too real. Might allow a flicker of hope to grow in his chest, leaving him open to a crushing fall if things didn't work out for the best. After all his work to keep any glimmer of hope at bay, creating channels for it to enter his system would be foolish.

She laid her cutlery on her empty plate and pushed it to the center of the table, her features neutral. "There will be a baby bump that will show through my clothes soon. How long are you thinking we keep everyone in the dark?"

He wanted to say, *Until we know for sure one way or the other,* but that would be an insensitive thing to say to an expectant mother. Instead he settled on a compromise and hoped she'd allow the sleight of hand. "We'll talk about it in the third trimester."

"Okay," she said and he could have sworn her eyes held a flash of relief. Was Pia as wary of announcing their news as he was? She stood and picked up her dishes, then paused. "If it's okay with you, I'll let Ryder and Seth know that you're lodging the claim today. To keep everything as fair and open as possible in this situation."

It grated to give any advantage, however slim, to the men who were blocking him from justice. Regardless that they'd probably find out during the day from their attorneys, for one unreasonable moment, he wanted Pia to stand by him. To choose *him* instead of choosing to be fair. But he brushed the feeling aside before it could take hold.

"Sure, why not," he said and picked up his empty plate.

The first thing Pia did when she got in to work that morning was conference call Ryder and Seth. Linda Adams was in court and this couldn't wait, although she made sure to leave Linda a message on her cell explaining the situation.

"Good morning, Ms. Baxter," Seth said. "I thought we were dealing with Ms. Adams now."

"In general you are, but I've had some advance warning that the claim to Warner Bramson's estate will be lodged today. Given the amount of media coverage that other developments in this case have generated, I thought you'd like to be prepared."

"Thanks," Ryder's voice rumbled. "I take it you garnered this information via your relationship with Hartley?"

"I did. And again, I assure you—"

"No need," Ryder interrupted.

"Thank you," she said, touched. "I appreciate it."

"And we appreciate that you shared this information," Seth said. "It's one advantage of having you close to the enemy. I'll alert my security and switchboard about the potential media interest."

After the call, she spent the morning in meetings, being briefed on anything she'd missed by not being in the office when she'd worked from home.

By the end of the day, the media had picked up on the development. Arthur came into her office and switched on the television. A news program had a reporter on the steps of the court, holding a large microphone in front of her face.

"No one's heard of JT Hartley before and his lawyer, a Philip Hendricks, tells us he won't be making any public comments. Our sources tell us Hartley's in property development and that his mother, Theresa Hartley, once worked for Bramson Holdings in the secretarial pool."

"Any word from Ryder Bramson or Seth Kentrell?" the news anchor asked.

"No, Jimmy. Despite repeated attempts to contact Warner Bramson's sons for comment, neither has been available. We'll continue trying and keep you up to date."

"Thanks, Angela." The screen switched to the news anchor. "Now we cross to one of JT Hartley's ex-employees who says—"

Pia clicked the television off. "So it's started," she said, almost to herself. Then she looked over at Arthur. "Thanks for letting me know."

Arthur nodded and headed for the door to his office. "The reception desk has had calls, too. I think the media are desperate for information."

As her assistant disappeared, Pia thought of JT at his office, probably with media swarming out front wanting a piece of him. The phone on her desk lured her to call and check on him, but *she'd* been the one to establish the new, stricter boundaries to their interactions. And for good reason.

Calling the man every time she thought about him

would mean she'd be ringing regularly. He could handle himself with the media, and he had a staff who she was sure would be well equipped to deal with anything that arose. JT was the father of her unborn child. That was all. And the sooner she accepted that, the better.

She noticed her hand was lightly caressing her stomach. Pulling it away, she picked up the files for a case that had nothing to do with Warner Bramson's offspring and determinedly put JT out of her mind.

Ten

The next day, Pia sat at her desk, attempting to blot out the world so she could simply get her work done. The night had been achingly lonely with only Winston to warm the bed. She'd lain for hours, staring at the wall, missing JT's presence as if she were missing a limb. The sheets still held his scent; her skin still held memories of his touch. Her body was hollowed out, empty, without him.

She paused in reading the second contract of the morning and slipped the pen between her teeth. She'd been right to insist JT leave yesterday—if she was this badly unsettled after only a few weeks with him in her bed, how would she have coped after a longer time? Developing a dependency on him had been one of her fears from the start and it seemed she'd just caught this one in time.

Her cell rang and when she reached for it, she saw JT's number. Her foolish heart leaped, and she laid a hand over her chest to steady it as she stared at the screen. Had she just congratulated herself on catching the dependency in time? She rolled her eyes at herself and pressed the talk button.

"Good morning, JT."

"Are you watching the news?" he asked with no preliminaries.

She looked down at the contract on her desk, with an ironic smile. "No, I'm busy trying to impress my boss and make partner."

"The media knows I was staying with you." His voice was strained, as if he was holding back the anger by only a tenuous thread.

A swarm of butterflies took flight in her belly. It was on the television? The entire world would know by the end of the day. Her parents, her sisters. JT's mother. JT's half brothers. She squeezed her eyes shut and whispered, "How?"

"Someone's leaked it. Maybe someone in your office who noticed my things when they dropped your work off, or just as easily a neighbor who recognized my face on the television," he said, voice weary. She could imagine him running fingers through his hair. "It hardly matters now."

Her heart sank into her stomach with a heavy thud as a realization hit. "I hadn't told my boss you were staying." She dropped her head into her hand. This would change the playing field. Change everything—who knew how Ted Howard would react?

"He'll know soon enough," JT said grimly. "But my main concern is your security. As you pointed out, anything to do with Warner Bramson's family has always been big news, and my being involved with someone from your firm has the undeniable scent of scandal attached. They'll have a feeding frenzy and I won't have you tracked down or your safety threatened."

Just at that moment, Ted Howard's secretary knocked on her open door, then dropped a note on her desk.

Ted wants you in his office as soon as you have a moment.

Bright panic flared in her chest, but she quickly tamped it down—if she didn't stay on top of the situation, she'd drown. "My boss just sent word he wants to see me," she said, adjusting her scarf with her free hand. "I have to go."

"Listen, I'm sending a car over to you tonight. I'd come myself, but that will make it worse."

Already planning what she'd say to Ted Howard, she blinked and had to replay JT's words. "A car? Why?"

"It'll be someone I trust to bring you to my place. Just grab Winston and what you need. We can send someone back for more of your things later."

Overloaded with thorny information, her temples began to throb. "You want me to move to your place when I'm in a hot vat of trouble over your staying at my place?"

"The media is going to camp out in front of your apartment," he said, voice adamant. "You don't have enough security to deal with them."

She'd watched the media go wild when JT's half brothers had become involved with women recently, but both those women had already been famous—Macy had grown up in the limelight as the daughter of a movie star and a business magnate, and April was a world-famous jazz singer. Sure, there was the angle of her working on the estate JT was claiming against, but it was hardly in the same league.

Her two priorities at the moment were her baby and her career. Her baby wouldn't be impacted by whether she went to JT's apartment or not, but her job most certainly would. It could make her situation at this firm even more precarious than it was already.

Her decision was plain—she couldn't go to JT.

"I appreciate your concern in making a plan to protect me, JT, but it won't be necessary."

"Pia, they're swarming," he said, voice deep. "But if you won't come to me, I'll have to insist on at least providing secure transport to your apartment. There will be a car waiting when you leave."

She looked down at the scrawled note on her desk from her boss's secretary and her stomach clenched. He was waiting for her. "Thank you, that's sweet, but I'm sorry, I have to go."

She straightened her jacket and smoothed her hair back, convincing herself she was ready for this meeting. That she had a chance of salvaging her career after the unacceptable mistakes she'd made. She would tell him everything, expose her actions and decisions as much as she needed to climb out of the hole she'd dropped herself in.

When she reached Ted Howard's reception room, his secretary smiled sympathetically. "He said you could go straight on in."

"Thanks, Margie." She took a deep breath and opened the door. Ted looked at her for a long moment over his glasses, then waved her into a seat.

"Is it true?" he asked.

She gave a short nod and interlaced her fingers over her crossed knees. "As you know, when I was working from home, it was on the doctor's recommendation for my safety. The doctor also recommended having someone in the apartment when I showered or did anything that would be dangerous if I fainted. JT was my only option. I have no family in town and he's the father of the baby. So he stayed at night. I ensured there was no paperwork pertaining to the case in the apartment when he was there."

Ted nodded and removed his glasses. "Pia, I have to

be honest. I've had some calls from clients who've seen the story on the news. They're worried about the firm's integrity."

Her mouth dried. She'd brought the firm into disrepute. Her lack of self-control around one man had created a domino effect that now had the potential to destroy so much.

She swallowed her pride and made the only offer she could see to fix the mess she'd created. "I'm prepared to take all my vacation time owing to carry me through to the start of maternity leave. With the extra months after the birth that the partners have approved, it should be enough time for the media interest and the speculation to have died down when I come back."

"That should help," Ted said, not missing a beat, obviously having considered this option already. "You should also know that when you come back from leave, things will be different. This has been a serious breach, Pia, and your new position will reflect that."

He *was* demoting her. "I understand," she said, her voice not much more than a croak.

"How long will it take you to hand your cases over?"

Digging her nails into her palms to keep from going numb, she checked her watch. Four-thirty. "I'll make a start now. I should have it all done by lunchtime tomorrow."

"Do it," he said, then looked back down at the papers on his desk, dismissing her with none of the professional esteem he'd given her until recently. Despite flinching at the sharp slap of the rejection, she had to acknowledge it was nothing more than appropriate for the person risking the firm's reputation, so she set her shoulders, ignored the sinking feeling in her stomach, and returned to her office.

The rest of the afternoon went by in a daze of handing cases to other lawyers and emptying her in-box. By the time she reached her building's foyer, she was almost drooping with mental exhaustion. Two security guards met her and explained JT had sent them, and that there were already journalists outside the building. Goose bumps erupted across her skin, so she thanked them and followed them through to the basement garage.

When they turned into her street, she saw a small group of journalists and photographers awaiting her on the sidewalk outside her apartment building and groaned. JT's warnings—and offer to stay with him—replayed in her mind, but she dismissed it, and when the media called out asking for a comment, she ignored them. The security escorted her to the door and saw her in before leaving. The idea of living in a fish bowl sent shivers across her skin, but as she'd told Ted Howard, it would die down soon enough.

As evening fell, even her bags of netting and ribbon couldn't distract her from the swelling group out front. With no response, they'd become more bold, and now there were regular knocks at her front-facing window. It had state-of-the-art security, so there was no physical threat, but she felt assaulted every time they called out.

"Pia, let us tell your side of the story!"

"Ms. Baxter, don't you want to set the record straight?"

Her pulse spiked each time there was a noise from outside. A voice in her head was telling her stress was bad for the baby, which made her worry more. She picked up Winston and curled up on the sofa with only one dim lamp. Seemed she'd underestimated the media interest.

Her phone rang until she pulled the cord out from the wall, and she turned music up to drown out the noise and the knowledge that they were there.

When her cell buzzed, she wanted to ignore it, but years of responding to the little piece of technology kicked in and she checked the number on the screen. JT's name flashed up and she trembled with relief. She thumbed the talk button and before he could try to convince her or say a word, she blurted, "Send the car back."

JT opened his door to find Pia with Winston in her arms, and two of the security team behind her, one carrying Pia's bags.

Her eyes were huge in her face, her skin too pale and he couldn't help but reach for her and enfold her in his arms. He'd been tormented by visions of her answering her door to the media and being confronted by a sea of camera flashes. Of a paparazzo carelessly jostling her and triggering a miscarriage. Of her being scared, and him not there to protect her. His chest had been too tight to take a full breath since the story had broken this afternoon.

He cleared his throat and spoke to the security men over her head. "Did you have any problems?"

The larger one shrugged as he put the bags down in the entranceway. "We've handled worse. Took her out a back entrance and around to a side street."

"I appreciate it." More than they could know. He held Pia tighter. There was a squirming against his chest as Winston struggled free and jumped down.

The men nodded and left to join the rest of the guards he'd hired this morning. JT would be making no public comment and wasn't taking a chance that the press would get close to him or Pia. Thankfully, now that she'd come to him, the guards would be able to keep a clearance zone around her and the vultures would have to try elsewhere to feed the public's morbid curiosity. They'd had their fill of Ryder's and Seth's lives, so the media's insatiable appetite for details of Warner Bramson's legacy was trained squarely on him and Pia.

After the door closed, Pia pulled back and he scanned her face. "Are you okay?"

"I am now." She looked down and a faint blush stole across her cheeks. "I don't know why a few reporters at my door would shake me up so much."

He could think of a number of reasons. Starting with how stressed she must be about her job. And being pregnant, responsible for the baby's well-being, had to make her feel more vulnerable. But he didn't want to remind her, so he smiled—albeit grimly—and picked up her bags. "It's your home—it's criminal that they can stalk you there. Anyone would have been stressed."

She flashed him a grateful smile and for a long minute he simply looked his fill—her copper waves hung loose around her shoulders, and were messily tumbled as if she'd just come from bed. Her fingers had probably twined through her hair from worry, but whatever had caused it, the effect was dramatic and beautiful and his hands wanted to touch. The last thing she needed after being rattled by the paparazzi was his coming on strong, so he clenched his fists around the handles of her bags and restrained the impulse.

"Come on through," he said and pointed to the wide archway that led into the living room. She walked in and slowly looked around, taking in the large flatscreen on the wall, and the distant views of the city lights through the open curtains.

What was she thinking? She'd known he'd done well financially, but the size and location of this apartment was irrefutable evidence of just how well. Was she surprised, being confronted with the transformation in fortunes of the outcast boy she'd befriended? Did she hate the dark color of the walls, the stark white trim?

She turned back to him and smiled. "This is nice." Her

voice was genuine and, stupidly, he felt like he'd been given some kind of award.

Shaking off the feeling, he put her bags on a low table and guided her to the L-shaped sofa. "What did your boss say about the media story?"

"I'm using up vacation time and starting maternity leave early." She sank down into the corner and tucked her feet underneath her. "I handed some things over today and just need to go in for a few hours in the morning."

She looked so despondent that he couldn't say what he was thinking—that it was probably for the best. He could keep her safe here, and she could take it easy for the rest of the pregnancy. It might not be great for her career, but a large part of him was glad.

He leaned back and rested his feet on the coffee table. "Did he mention the promotion?"

"It's off the table." She grimaced. "In fact, I'll be demoted when I go back."

"I'm sorry." He took her hand, intending to offer comfort, but as soon as her palm slid against his, his pulse fractured.

Pia looked down at their tangled fingers. "When I go back to work after the leave, I'll keep my head down and work like crazy. It won't be in the time frame I'd hoped, but I'll still make partner."

Seeing the determination in her eyes, his chest swelled with pride. "Good for you."

Winston came running into the room and skidded to a halt on the tiled floor. He looked around, then vanished down a hallway, investigating his new environment. Pia smiled, glad at least one of them could treat this as an adventure.

She turned back to JT, the man who'd rescued her

tonight, and gave him a smile, too. "So how was your day?"

"Better than yours," he said with a trace of humor in his eyes. "Thankfully I'm my own boss."

"I'm beginning to see the advantages of that arrangement." JT had more responsibility riding on his shoulders, sure, but because the company's fate came down to him, the thrill of success must be more satisfying. A definite advantage that being in business had over her line of work and for one liberated minute, she envied him.

"Did you hear from Bramson's sons?" JT asked, interrupting her thoughts.

Pia hesitated. The speculation was that she would be feeding JT information about the case. So should she be wary of doing exactly that now? Though, the only contact she'd had with Warner Bramson's other sons was yesterday when she'd given *them* an advantage she'd gained from knowing JT. And she'd warned JT that morning she'd be calling them, so it was only fair to tell him she'd done that.

She nodded. "I rang them yesterday morning and gave them a heads-up so they could get any extra measures in place to screen the media interest if they needed."

There were more questions in his eyes, but he refrained from asking them, and she appreciated it.

"You know, I think we both need a night off," he said, standing and resting his hands low on his hips.

She thought of the paparazzi that had been hovering outside her apartment and she shivered. "We can't go out."

"Then we'll make do with what we have here." He seemed unconcerned by the prospect of being cooped up in his own place, but then, this room was almost bigger than her entire apartment.

She looked around speculatively. "What *do* we have here?"

"A penthouse suite designed to my specifications," he said with a crooked grin.

The man who dealt in property every day had created his own apartment? Suddenly she was very interested to see what he'd designed. "Okay, show me what you've got."

Eyes flashing with the challenge and innuendo, he reached out a hand and helped her up. Twenty minutes later, after she'd seen the theater room, the conservatory, the million-dollar views of the night skyline and the spa room, he guided her through another doorway.

"This is the library." And sure enough, the walls were lined with shelves of books on three sides, but the fourth side had something altogether different. A motorbike mounted on the wall. A familiar bike.

"That's it," she breathed. The bike he'd built when they were teenagers. The one he'd whipped her away on regularly. The one they'd ridden to the beach where she'd given JT her virginity.

It was cleaner than she'd ever seen it, the chrome gleaming, the tires jet-black. She reached out and touched the spokes of the front wheel. It was like JT—the same as before but different.

"Yep, that's it," he said, his voice tinged with nostalgia.

She stepped back to better see the entire bike at once, and found JT behind her. He wrapped his arms around her waist and she leaned into his solid, warm chest. "I can't believe you've kept it all these years."

She felt him shrug broad shoulders. "It reminds me of where I came from. Reminds me never to take what I have now for granted."

Very sensible. Not at all where *her* thoughts had roamed. "It reminds me of riding on the back of it," she said, her voice rougher around the edges than she would have liked. She remembered being pressed against him, her thighs tightly wrapped around his hips, breasts pushed into his back, arms clinging to his torso. A flash of heat spread across her skin.

He ran a blunt fingertip from her shoulder down her arm. "It took us to some great places."

"*You* took us to some great places."

"I didn't care where I was," he said softly, turning her to face him, "as long as you were there with me."

Looking into his vivid green eyes, she was flooded by the feelings, the yearnings, of her sixteen-year-old self. "I loved you so much back then," she whispered.

He looked away, up at the bike, and said fiercely, "You were my whole world."

Her heart felt as if it were tearing in two for everything they'd lost, and tears filled her eyes even as she tried to blink the dampness away. "I miss that feeling."

"I think it's something only the young can feel," he said, gaze still on the bike. "When you're still full of naïveté and optimism."

The words themselves were heartrending, but his tone was so melancholy that she could barely stand it. And the worst part was, she believed him. Nothing in her life had ever come close to the teenaged passion she'd had for this man.

"So we'll never have it again with anyone else?" she asked, afraid she already knew the answer.

His gaze fell back to her, eyes burning with intense, unreadable emotion. "I know I won't."

JT watched emotions tumble over each other on Pia's face. Then her bottom lip quivered as she drew in a breath. "Can we try and reclaim it—just for one night?"

Last night had been torture—and it had only been a single night apart. He'd gone for a late-night ride to release some of the tension, but then he'd realized his bike had been his first response when Pia had left him fourteen years ago. Annoyed with himself, he'd turned for home. This was *nothing* like then. He'd been a teenager desperately in love.

This time he was a man who simply missed spending his nights with one particular woman. *Missed them beyond measure.* And didn't that just reinforce what she'd said at the restaurant?

He cleared his throat. "You said we needed to be careful about falling into a marriage by default, and you were right."

"It's only one night," she said quietly, tentatively, as if she knew he'd say no. "One last time."

He watched her sensual mouth as she spoke and his skin tightened. It was as if he was addicted and another night with her would be his fix. And that would mean starting the withdrawal from scratch again once it was over. He'd made it through the first night; theoretically, it should be easier from here—it'd be madness to put himself back on the starting blocks.

Although with her in his arms, her darkened violet eyes looking up at him, his body burning with need for her, he shuddered with the effort of not pulling her close. "We're playing with fire—you told me so yourself. How would it be any easier to stop tomorrow than it is now?"

Her forehead puckered and her tongue touched her top lip as she considered. "I don't know if it's the right thing or the wrong thing. But after the paparazzi, the mad scramble leaving my apartment, feeling that everything is unraveling no matter what I do…"

He threaded his fingers through the luscious firefall of her hair and unable to resist, he feathered a kiss over her forehead. "What about the dangers?"

"I know, I know," she said, her eyes tortured. "But, JT, I

need you to hold me tonight." She laid a hand on his chest and it seared even through his shirt.

It's only one night. One last time.

The words were like a drumbeat in his head. He dragged in a sharp breath and made a silent vow to make it special.

Eleven

As JT lowered his head and took her mouth, desire ripped through him like a flash fire. Sensations threatened to overwhelm—he locked his muscles and stilled, attempting to wrest back control, but she writhed impatiently against him.

"Please, JT," she said, her voice almost a whimper.

Of its own volition, his body loosened and he pulled her close—he'd never been able to deny her much of anything. Withstanding demands and playing his own game was pretty much his business model, and it came easy to him. With everyone except Pia—he'd never had any defenses against Pia saying please.

He wrapped her left leg around his hips. Pressing her against the wall, he lifted her other knee so she could link her ankles behind him. The core of her pressed over his erection and he shuddered—even through their clothes, he could feel the siren's call of heat.

With her shoulders braced on the wall behind her, her breasts were laid out before him like a banquet. He traced fingertips down the sides and underneath their fullness, then up to lightly graze their peaks through the fabric of her clothes. A rosy bloom crept up her neck to her cheeks as her breathing grew labored.

Her eyelids fluttered closed. "How far to your room?"

He drew in a sharp breath, forcing his brain to work. "Down the hall."

"Too far." She began to unbutton his shirt.

She was right—the bed seemed continents away with her fingers fluttering against the sensitized skin of his chest as she worked to remove the shirt. But hadn't he just vowed to make this special for her?

"I'll walk quickly," he said and pulled her against him. He strode down the long hallway, Pia kissing and nipping at his neck the whole way, testing his resolve not to take her before they reached the master bedroom.

They made it to his bed and she released her legs but he held her high against him for extra moments, savoring the warm, silken feel of her. Then he let her slide slowly down, until her feet reached the floor, and he caught her mouth in a hungry kiss.

He'd dreamed of this moment—over the years and even recently. Sharing *her* bed had been one thing, but having her in his apartment, beside *his* bed, brought out something deep down inside of him. Something proud and primal. *Mine.*

His legs shook with the power of the thought, and he sank to the side of the bed, pulling her to stand in the V of his thighs. He looked up into her passion-darkened gaze. He'd never wanted her more than he did in this moment.

He removed the pieces of her trouser suit one at a time, forcing himself to go slowly, savoring the sight of each new glimpse of flesh. He'd always loved her lush, rounded body, but now, with her belly ripening, she was so beautiful that a ball of emotion lodged in his throat.

He skimmed his hands from her hips down, taking her panties with them, and as she stepped from them, she steadied herself with hands on his shoulders. The touch burned through his shirt.

"Princess," he rasped. He splayed hands across her hips and drew her closer, and when her body was pressed against his, her nails dug into his shoulders, driving him a little crazier.

He laid her back on the bed, then toed off his shoes, stripped off his clothes and found a condom in record time, but even those seconds away from her felt like torture.

He covered her with his body, bracing his forearms on the cool sheets either side of her shoulders. The press of their bodies, the touch of skin, was heavenly. Despite the insistent protests of his body, he wanted to linger, simply feeling their bodies touching chests to toes.

Until she ground up against him.

Then all bets were off. He entered the slick heat of her and a tremor ripped through his body.

Pia.

He began moving in long, slow glides and her hands fisted in the sheets. The feel of her enveloping him like a glove made it almost impossible to hold on, to not end this too soon like an inexperienced teenager. In some ways, the intensity of this time being their last, made it feel like their first time—desperate to touch, to make memories out of sensation.

Her hands left the sheets to hold him low on his hips, pulling him closer, meeting each stroke. Her skin was like fire on his—how could he ever want more than this? He snaked a hand down between them to find the place she ached most.

She broke, and hearing his name on her lips, the spasms of her body, took him from the edge of ecstasy all the way over and into free fall.

Pia sat at her desk on her final day at the firm before she took leave, her chest cramping tight. How had things come to this? Security guards had to sneak her out of JT's apartment building this morning and bring her in. She was pregnant and single. She was holding on to her career by only the most tenuous of threads. She should be basking in the hope and optimism of impending motherhood. Instead, her life was in shambles.

She'd handed some of her work over yesterday, and only had a few things to tidy up this morning before she could leave. Including a few boxes of Warner Bramson's papers that she needed to pass onto Arthur now that he would be assisting Linda Adams on the case. She knelt down beside one, and flicked through the pages. It was the rest of the paperwork from Warner's locked office cupboard. The boxes she'd already sorted had mainly been financial accounts for both his families, old reports on long-past ventures, and notes on potential business moves. There were only these two boxes left to sift through—a task she didn't regret handing over after already sorting through twenty-three similar boxes before she fell pregnant. She picked up a wad of papers from the first box to straighten them and moved to put them back in when she saw the word *Hartley.* Her heart jumped into her throat as the pages in her hand spilled across the floor.

The piece of paper was old and yellowed and filled her entire vision.

The child, James Theodore Hartley, is now three years

old and living in Kentucky. His mother is working as a waitress at a local diner. When questioned about the boy's father, she became agitated and reported that he was dead. I believe the chances that she'll reappear and make claims are slim.

It was a short, one-page report, with an out-of-focus photo of JT as a small boy stapled to the back.

She quickly flicked to the next page in the pile. Another report, this time of a four-year-old JT. Pulse thundering, she searched the scattered pages on the floor and found the two reports before these. Further into the box were years' worth of updates, until just last year.

Her skin iced over as she realized the implications. If Warner had known about JT, then JT couldn't make a claim under New York law—Warner had left him out of the will on purpose, not because he hadn't known of his existence. JT's claim against Warner Bramson's will was over. She closed her eyes and sat back on her heels. JT would be crushed. Devastated. Everything he'd been working toward, gone in a matter of minutes.

Her insides constricted, as if even her body was rebelling against what she had to do. She'd give anything not to have to tell him this; never in her career had conveying information felt so *wrong*. One thing she knew: She had to tell him in person, somewhere private.

But before she could leave the office, Ryder and Seth needed to know—should she let Linda Adams tell them? She'd called the brothers two days ago to give them advance warning of the claim being lodged, but that wasn't something she was doing in a strictly professional capacity—she'd come by the information privately and was passing it on as a courtesy. This, however, was information regarding the estate. *The information that would end JT's claim.*

No, if anyone was going to deliver this information to Warner Bramson's sons, she wanted it to be her.

She slipped into Linda's office and showed her the documents.

"Would you mind if I was the one to ring the beneficiaries and tell them?" Pia asked.

"Sure," Linda said with a quick nod. "One less thing for me to do after you go."

Back in her own office, Pia asked her secretary to organize a conference call with Ryder and Seth immediately and sat at her desk to read through the private investigator reports until the call was ready. They charted JT's passage through childhood—the progression of towns, starting to get into trouble with the police in a couple of places before they moved on. And all the while, his rich, powerful, *rotten* father was watching from afar, doing *nothing.*

The buzz from her phone told her the call was ready. She locked down the dangerous cocktail of emotions swirling through her body and took a breath. After greeting JT's brothers, she said, "I have news about the claim."

"I hope it's good news," Ryder said. "The media photographers are annoying Macy."

Pia closed her eyes and plunged in. "I've uncovered evidence that Warner knew of JT Hartley's existence."

Two sharply indrawn breaths came down the line.

"What kind of evidence?" Seth asked.

She looked at the papers covering her desk. "Private investigator reports. They were filed once a year, and cover from when he was a baby until last year."

"Well, I'll be damned," Ryder said.

Everything inside her braced—as if this were her own dream she was shattering, not JT's—and she forced the words out through numb lips. "You realize what this means?"

"His claim is over," Ryder said bluntly. "Good work."

"Thank you, Pia," Seth said. "And I appreciate that you've done this under difficult circumstances."

She knew what Seth was referring to—there was no way they would have missed the juicy tidbits of gossip about her living with JT—but she didn't, couldn't reply. Not when her body was heavy with the knowledge she was destroying JT's claim for his rightful inheritance.

She said goodbye, rang off and on autopilot, called Arthur in to give him the boxes. Then she told Linda Adams the calls had been made and handed her the final case notes, cleared out her top drawer, bid her secretary farewell for the next few months and picked up the phone.

JT answered on the first ring. "Are you okay?" he asked.

His voice flowed over her like a soothing balm, but she was about to shatter everything he was working toward. Would he change toward her? Shoot the messenger?

She swallowed. "I'm fine, but I have something to tell you. How soon can you meet me at your place?"

"I'll leave now and meet you there," he said without hesitation.

With a sick feeling in her belly, she hung up and went to meet the security in the foyer to take her to JT's apartment.

JT arrived home in record time, body tense about what Pia would have to tell him. He'd immediately ruled out a miscarriage because she would have called him to the hospital or to wherever she was. But that still left a whole raft of possibilities: Maybe she'd had word from Dr. Crosby that one of the tests had found something wrong with their child. The media had pushed her too far and she was leaving town. As he considered each possibility, more jumped into his mind.

When he opened the door to her ten minutes later, he had trouble not leaping on her. “Are you all right?” he asked, taking her briefcase. “The baby?”

“We’re both safe. The news is about you.” She said the words slowly, watching him intently as she did. “How about we sit down?”

“How about you tell me here,” he said, putting her briefcase on the tiles and folding his arms over his chest. If the news was about him, he wasn’t prepared to waste time getting comfortable.

She nodded, her face pale. “I found something in Warner’s paperwork today.”

The air surrounding them seemed to still as he did the math—the news was about him plus a discovery in Warner’s paperwork. “He had papers about me.” He heard his voice as if from a distance, flat and hard.

Pia’s tongue darted out to moisten her lips. “Private investigator reports.”

“How many?” he asked as the room began to slowly revolve around them. Everything he knew about his life was changing, he could feel it deep in his bones.

“Starting when you were a baby—” she hesitated, swallowed “—filed every year, up until last year.”

“He was still having me followed last year?” Bitter rage rose and filled his chest to bursting point. That man had deliberately cut him and his mother off from financial support when he was alive *and* when he was dead, yet he’d paid some investigator to stalk them? His lungs labored but he still couldn’t get enough air.

Soft fingers intertwined with his and tugged him deeper into the apartment. He sank down into the couch and felt her sit beside him.

"I'm sorry about the claim," she whispered, her voice gentle.

He frowned as the cogs in his brain turned to process her words. The claim. It had no legal standing and was over. That hardly rated right now. This slimy man who'd sired him had had him followed his entire life. Knew exactly what circumstances he and his mother lived in. *Warner Bramson had known that the woman he'd impregnated was struggling.* And he'd done nothing but use it as entertainment. Bile ate into his gut. He wished to hell Warner Bramson was still alive so he could confront him face to face. Or maybe fist to face.

"I've changed my mind," he said through a jaw clenched tight. "I wouldn't take a cent of that man's tainted money."

"JT—"

He cut her off and steered the subject away—his rage was too raw for her to take the brunt on that topic. "I assume you've told his sons?" he said, moderating his voice as much as he could.

"I rang Ryder and Seth, then came home here to tell you."

He stood and stalked to the floor-to-ceiling window. His body trembled with the need to do something. To ride until he ran out of gas. To find a gym with a punching bag. But they weren't options he could take up while Pia was here. He wouldn't walk out on her. Calling on every ounce of his self-discipline, he reined in his anger and focused on Pia. This was no picnic in the park for her either and he wouldn't lose sight of that. He turned to find her behind him, waiting, her arms wrapped around herself.

"I'm sorry, princess," he said tightly.

Her eyes flared wide and her arms dropped to her sides. "Why are you sorry?"

"Your career is in tatters, everything is a mess." *He'd made it into a mess.* "And it was all for nothing."

"It wasn't for nothing," she said, her delicate hand reaching to cup his cheek. "You finally know who your father was. You'd always wanted to know that."

He squeezed his eyes shut, unwilling to give in to the rage now that he had some control over it. "I preferred not knowing to finding out it was this monster."

"There's something else I should tell you," she said tentatively.

His shoulders stiffened. What else could there possibly be? "Go on."

She took a small step back and folded her arms under her breasts. "It wasn't a coincidence I had this account."

"Warner gave it to you?" He eyed her sharply. "Did he know of our involvement?" He wouldn't put it past that twisted man to try and manipulate people from beyond the grave.

"I don't think he knew." Her forehead creased as she considered. "At least there was nothing in the reports about me."

"So why do you have it?" he asked warily.

"I asked for it," she said, and drew in a shaky breath. "Lobbied for it, actually."

His jaw slackened as he put the pieces of the puzzle together. The betrayal slugged him right in the solar plexus. "You *knew?*"

"I suspected," she said, wincing. "You mother slipped once over lunch and mentioned the name Warner. It's not a common name and the first Warner who came to mind was powerful enough to keep Theresa on the run over the years. So I did a little digging."

He shoved his fingers through his hair and forced

himself to relax. Pia hadn't known, merely suspected. Not a betrayal. "Did she know you were doing that?"

"I never said a word. But I found out she worked in the Bramson Holdings' secretarial pool about the time you were conceived. It wasn't much, and purely circumstantial, but enough to convince me I could be right."

He sank his hands into his pockets. He had to be missing something here. "But still, why take on the case?"

"I thought…hoped, I could do something. For Theresa, and for you." She drifted over to a framed photo of his mother on a shelf and picked it up, touching the glass with a finger.

He moved behind her and looked down at the photo she held. It was one of his favorite snapshots—his mother laughing at something he'd said. Even with everything she'd had to cope with, she always made sure he'd never felt the strain she'd been under. The woman deserved a medal.

He looked back at Pia—she'd also tried to help, but taking on his father's will and estate was at best misguided. "What could you have done?"

Shrugging one shoulder, she replaced the photo but didn't meet his eyes. "I nudged a few times on the question of heirs. Asked if there was the possibility of other children we needed to allow for when we drew up the will."

He choked out a laugh. "He denied it, of course. Point-blank denied my existence."

She nodded. Didn't need to say the words. "I'm sorry," she said, then chewed down on her bottom lip. "I know this seems like I was sticking my nose into your family business, but—"

"But you were trying to help my mother," he finished for her. A week ago he might have been more upset about the interference. But between the media stalking them and discovering his father was a monster who'd tracked him through years of childhood and never lifted a finger to help, he couldn't work up too much steam for this as well.

"Yes," she said weakly.

He rubbed a hand across his chin, looking for his equilibrium. "I can't fault your motives, but I wish you'd come to me instead of setting off on your own."

"We weren't on friendly terms, JT."

She was right—would he have even spoken with her a year ago? His cell rang in his pocket. His gut clenched. Could it be worse timing? He'd turn the damn thing off and let it take messages. But as he fished it out, he saw his office's private line and his heart sank.

"I have to take this," he said, glancing up at Pia. "It's my secretary and I told her to only call if it was urgent."

Pia smiled her understanding and walked over to Winston who was perched on a vacant shelf in the bookcase. JT watched her draw the cat to her chest and felt a stab of jealousy over the easy way she cuddled him. He rolled his eyes—things were sad if he was jealous of a feline.

Bracing an arm against the wall, he thumbed the talk button. "Hello, Mandy."

"I'm sorry to interrupt, Mr. Hartley, but there's something new on the internet news that I thought you'd want to know."

Still watching Pia and Winston, he shook his head. Probably his half brothers crowing over their win. "It's okay, Mandy, I know about the loss of standing—"

"Mr. Hartley, they're saying Ms. Baxter is pregnant. By you."

He swore and covered his eyes with a hand as the world crowded in on him.

* * *

Pia grabbed her ringing cell from her bag, just as she heard JT let loose an oath. Her screen showed Seth Kentrell. In her rush to leave the office, she'd forgotten to tell him and Ryder Bramson that she wouldn't be around. At least this should be a quick call.

She answered, plastering a professional smile on her face so it would come through in her voice. "Mr. Kentrell, I should have told you before, but I'm on leave as of today. All issues need to go through Linda Adams now."

"Maternity leave?" he asked, his tone giving nothing away.

She gasped, and Winston, always sensitive to changes, jumped down. How had Seth found out? And more important, how much did he know?

"Ah, yes," she stammered. "It is."

"I saw a report on the web claiming you're pregnant. It's Hartley's, isn't it? I guess that's what you meant by a conflict of interests."

Panic swirled through her body and perspiration broke out on her forehead. Her eyes flicked to JT as he listened to his secretary, the same look of shell shock on his face that she felt inside. He'd heard it, too. It appeared there was no way to contain this. Only one course of action remained. "Mr. Kentrell, I am very sorry. I can explain—"

"No need," he said, dismissing her apology. "I merely wanted to let you know I'm impressed with your integrity."

There was no sarcasm in his tone, but there could be no other reason for this call than censure. "Again, I'm sorry."

"You had a chance to destroy those PI reports, Pia. The father of your baby would still have a claim—one we were pretty sure he'd win."

Her lips parted as she finally understood his meaning—

he really *had* called to commend her ethics—but then she frowned. "I didn't have a choice."

"We always have choices. You could have protected him."

"By destroying evidence? That's a crime." The very thought of it made her shudder.

"If he'd won, some of the money could have filtered down to your child," Seth persisted.

Violate her ethics for money? Her spine straightened. "I'm simply not built that way."

"I can see that," Seth said, warm approval in his voice. "Previously, I had a good opinion of you, but you've just shot up in my estimation. If you ever need anything, you let me know."

"I appreciate it," she said, a little dazed, and hung up.

JT had already ended his call and watched her from his spot on the carpet, his back against the wall. "Seems the word is out," he said mildly, belying the tension around his eyes.

She pinched the bridge of her nose and let out a breath. The ramifications of this news breaking publicly were too far reaching to even comprehend, starting with Theresa Hartley—

Her heart swooped. "JT, your *mother*."

His eyes closed and he swore again. Then he reached for his cell and dialed, and she tapped out her parents' number on her own phone.

An hour later, Pia was reeling. She sank down onto the couch near JT and watched him stretch his arms over his head. The fabric of his cotton business shirt pulled taut against his torso and her breath caught. Resisting the urge to reach out and touch the muscular lines, she turned away.

"How did your calls go?" he asked.

Tiring, she thought, and sighed. "My parents were

disapproving and self-righteous. So nothing unusual there. How was your mother?"

He grimaced. "Worried about the media coverage. Thrilled about the baby. Worried that you'll break my heart again. Thrilled that you're back on the scene." A weary, crooked grin spread across his face. "She's compared every girl I've ever had on my arm to you."

Theresa was lovely. Pia smiled. One of the best things to come from this pregnancy was formalizing her relationship with Theresa for life.

You'll love your Grandma Theresa, little one.

She looked back at JT, curiosity getting the best of her. "Have there been many girls on your arm?"

"None for more than three or four nights." He said the words simply—no trace of shame or pride, merely stating the facts.

At the restaurant, he'd said he preferred to keep things uncomplicated with women, and she'd assumed from that he didn't let them close. But this was something different again. She'd imagined two or three long-term girlfriends kept at an emotional arm's length, not a string of women who weren't even around long enough to call it a relationship.

"You haven't had a relationship since we broke up?" she asked tentatively.

"I learned I'm not fond of relationships. Thanks for that insight, by the way." His eyes weren't bitter; in fact, they held wry amusement.

She didn't smile back—how could she when the future held no chance of bonds forming with his half brothers, no wife and family apart from their baby? Everything inside her *ached* for JT to be happy in his life.

"Surely you'll have a long-term relationship someday?"

"Never again," he said with certainty, then changed the subject. "Who were your other calls?"

"One was Ted Howard, my boss."

"Checking up on you?" he asked.

"Firing me." She flinched as she said it, but was thankful for small mercies—having the same conversation in person would have been a hundred times harder. Seeing the disappointment in Ted's eyes as he expressed his regrets on how things had turned out when he'd had such high hopes for her future. Having to walk away, then through the firm's corridors instead of simply hanging up.

JT's face darkened. "He fired you?"

"He's in damage control." She couldn't blame Ted. Her actions had put him in a tight corner and he'd had to act. "Every person in the city knows I slept with you and that I'm pregnant. His clients were demanding he fire me or they'd walk."

"I'm sorry, Pia," he said, voice ragged.

She shrugged one shoulder, trying for nonchalance but likely failing. "He had no choice. He also pointed out that I'd probably have to go interstate to practice law when I'm ready to go back to work."

He reached for her hand and held it firmly. "It'll blow over. People will forget." His tone was reassuring but his eyes held doubt.

"Lawyers have long memories. Partners at other firms will feel they can never trust me." And if she started over somewhere else, then any gains she'd made on her professional reputation would be lost. She'd been *so* close to making partner, and now her legal career was back at square one. Law might not have been her first choice of a profession, but she'd thrown everything she had into it. And fallen short.

"You can work for me," JT said decisively. "I have a large legal department."

Despite being touched by his white knight attempt, she grinned at the irony. "Oh yeah, that's the solution. Intertwine our lives even more because it's worked out so well this far."

He chuckled, his face relaxing for the first time since she'd walked in the door. "I guess you're right. But listen, don't worry about money and the baby. I swear I'll always make sure you're both provided for."

She had no doubt of that. He was nothing like his father—JT would never leave her and the baby to struggle, she knew that in her heart. He was a good man, JT Hartley. Yet fate had dealt him an unfair blow today in destroying his chances to claim against his father's will. She needed to do something to rectify that.

And suddenly she knew exactly what to do.

Twelve

Pia sat in Ryder Bramson's large office, moonlight streaming in through the tall windows. Her pulse echoed through her body on every beat as she looked around at the gathered people. Ryder sat to her right, holding tight to Macy's hand. Seth was opposite them, his arm around April.

The office vibrated with the tension of people who rarely sat in the same room. As far as she knew, Ryder and Seth had only joined forces once—against JT. At the thought of JT, her heart lit a stubborn flame. She'd told him she needed to go out and he hadn't questioned her, had merely arranged for the security guards to accompany her and checked she had her phone. He'd said he had an appointment of his own. She'd left and quickly made the calls to organize this meeting. Luckily everyone had been able to make it on short notice.

Her hands trembled in her lap. This could either go well

or end in disaster—and she'd lose the good will of the only business people left in New York who trusted her. But she was willing to gamble the remnants of her professional reputation. For JT. For the future of their child.

She cleared her throat. "Thank you for coming."

Ryder nodded. "We owed you. Telling us about the private investigator reports despite your connections to Hartley took integrity."

"Not to mention the heads-up you gave us the day his challenge was lodged," Seth added.

Macy smiled encouragingly. "But you said on the phone you're not working for that firm anymore?"

"No," Pia said. "They fired me." It'd only been a few hours ago, but already the sting was wearing off. In its place was a feeling strangely similar to…freedom.

"What?" Ryder said at the same time Seth said, "There's a job working for me, anytime you want it."

Pia's eyes stung with tears at the unexpected job offer and its implicit support. These men—JT's brothers—were magnificent, noble men. Like JT himself.

"Thank you," she said and meant it. "But I didn't ask for a meeting to discuss my employment."

Ryder leaned forward in his chair. "Perhaps you should tell us why you did request it, then."

She nodded and drew in a shaky breath. Showtime. She had one chance at this, to get it right. If things didn't go to plan, their resistance would deepen and prevent a second opportunity. There was no room for failure.

"Ryder," she said, looking him in the eye, "Macy is what? Seven months pregnant?"

"Six," he said with a glow lighting him from within. He turned to Macy and a look passed between them of such love and beauty that Pia's heart ached.

"Tell me," Pia said, finding her voice again, "what would you do for that baby?"

As his chest expanded, Ryder's eyes took on a formidable glint. "She's the most important thing in the world. I'd do anything for her."

Pia's glaze flicked to Macy. Ryder had said "her." "You're having a girl?"

Macy placed a hand over her swollen belly. "Yes, we are. Georgia."

A ball of emotion lodged in Pia's throat. She had a scan booked for next week when she'd find out her baby's gender and suddenly, she was desperate to know. But more than knowing the sex of the baby, she wished she had with JT what Macy had with Ryder. JT had been to her appointments and was more supportive than a woman could hope, but she wanted it *all.* She wanted breakfasts together and nights in his bed. She wanted to see his face light up when he was happy and comfort him when he was down. She wanted to be held in his arms and to have more of his children.

Oh, God, she *loved* him.

The earth tilted to the side. Loved him as much as she ever had. More—it was rooted deep in her heart. How had she kept herself blind to this?

"Pia, are you all right?" Macy asked.

"Sorry," she said, gathering herself with great effort and focusing back on the plan, then turning to Seth. "Forgive me, but would it be intrusive to ask if you and April plan on children?"

With eyebrows raised, Seth looked to April, who nodded assent. "Yes, we're planning on having children," he said.

Pia couldn't restrain a sentimental smile. Whether this plan worked or not, more cousins for her baby were being planned right this minute. She laced her fingers and met

Seth's gaze again. "When you have those babies, how far do you think you would go for them?"

Seth didn't hesitate. "No limits—a father should put his children first. Always act in their best interests." His eyes hardened. "If I learned nothing else from my childhood, it's that children should never be treated as afterthoughts."

Ryder's eyes flashed as he met his half brother's midnight-blue gaze. The air was suddenly electric, resonating with power, with understanding. Pia had a feeling that they'd just connected in a way they never had before. There was silence in the room, as if everyone was aware that something fundamental had changed.

"Thank you for your honesty," she finally said to Seth. Then she looked at each man in turn. "I've been working with and watching your family for some time now. Seen the pressures you're under, seen some of the challenges you face, and if you'll excuse the audacity—" she drew in a lungful of air "—your father didn't support and protect either of you, the way you will your children. Although he made sure you had the things you needed while you were growing up, he put you in difficult circumstances all your lives, then pitted you against each other with his will."

The room was still, as if no one could quite believe she'd said the words aloud. *She* couldn't believe she'd said them, and just prayed this hadn't made things worse between the brothers. She saw Seth's eyes flick to Ryder, then away again, and Ryder look down at where his daughter was cradled in Macy's womb. Macy squeezed his hand, but still no one spoke, so Pia plunged on into the void.

"And he did even worse by JT. He followed his firstborn son's progress from the time he was a little boy, during the nomadic life his mother was forced to lead, and all through his troubled teens. Warner was aware of the struggle that Theresa Hartley had as a single mother and yet he did nothing. Less than nothing—he was so set on keeping JT out in the cold that he paid an investigator to keep track of them for decades, making sure they weren't a threat to him rather than try to offer the tiniest bit of help."

Ryder's brows shot up. "Does Hartley know you're doing this?"

"No, he doesn't," she said, praying JT would understand when she told him. She looked at the thoughtful look on each man's face, could see the likeness to JT in the expressions on their faces, the pensive narrowing of their eyes. They were obviously thinking about her words, weighing them—the same way JT did when she challenged him. At least they weren't dismissing her out of hand. Her heart squeezed painfully with a tiny glow of hope.

"I'm having JT's baby and I know he'll do everything in his power to ensure our child has a good life—the same way that you'll both do for your children. You're good men. The three of you. You're not like your father. Warner spent his whole life keeping you all isolated in different ways."

As she watched them, tears in her eyes, Pia felt a tightness across her belly. She waited, holding her breath, but there was no other sensation, so she relaxed again.

She gathered her thoughts and looked back to them. "Please don't let his death compound that wrong. I want my baby to know its family. *All* of its family."

"So do I." Macy ran a hand over her belly as she stood. She crossed to Pia and hugged her.

"Me too, Pia," April said, joining them. Then she whispered in Pia's ear, "Thank you."

Pia felt a tear run down her cheek. These strong, loving women would make sure her baby would know its cousins. And hopefully one day that would pave the way for JT to have a relationship with his brothers. He didn't want her love, but she could give him this.

They turned to look at the two men still seated who eyed each other warily, like two lions circling. Pia held her breath and had the sense that Macy and April were doing the same. Then the men nodded almost infinitesimally, in some male code.

"We're outnumbered," Seth murmured, a wry smile on his lips.

"And outgunned," Ryder said. "But they're right. Maybe it is time to bury the hatchet."

Seth sighed and nodded. "Maybe it's past time." He stood and held out his hand. "To be frank, it was never our hatchet."

Ryder took the offered hand and shook once before sitting back down. "Besides, I've a hankering to meet our brother. I'm suddenly more of a family man than I realized."

Macy smiled broadly, her arm still around Pia. "And JT must be someone very special—Pia loves him."

A spasm flashed across Pia's belly again and she gasped. April touched her arm and looked into her eyes. "Are you okay?"

Pia shrugged one shoulder, telling herself that it wasn't a problem, wasn't like fourteen years ago, but her heart was racing. "I'm fine. I've just been having some twinges."

"It's probably Braxton-Hicks contractions," Macy said, reassuringly.

"I think you're right." She *hoped* she was right.

They moved back to their chairs, then another twinge hit and panic flared in every nerve and cell of her body. Her hands went to her stomach, terrified that she knew what it meant. This couldn't be happening. It was too early. *Too early.* Her breath came in short, sharp gasps. Darkness and memories of that night fourteen years ago threatened to engulf her, but she struggled to keep her head above them, to keep control of her mind so she could protect her baby.

Macy put an arm around her shoulders.

Pia didn't even try to hide her fear. "I lost JT's baby once before. It was at the same point, and there's a risk it'll happen again." *No,* she wanted to scream. *Don't let this happen.*

Ryder was on his feet and behind his desk. "I'll get an ambulance."

Seth reached for Pia's cell, where it lay beside her bag. "I'll call Hartley."

Two hours later, Pia was in a hospital bed, undergoing tests, more terrified than she'd been since she was sixteen. They hadn't been able to reach JT—his cell was switched off, and his secretary had refused to disclose his whereabouts to his half brothers. Her gaze darted around the stark room, her heart fluttering against her ribs. She'd been trying to hold her fears in check, but it was only the flimsiest of barricades that prevented them from flooding her. Seth and Ryder were out in the waiting room, and April and Macy had stayed with her, but she wanted only JT. His voice would soothe her more than the doctors' calm smiles, his presence would lend her more strength than Macy and April's carefully chosen words.

JT, where are you?

There was a sharp knock at the door and Seth's head appeared. April slipped over to him for a whispered conversation, then came rushing back and turned on the small television.

A reporter's face filled the screen. "As I said before the break, we've managed to secure an exclusive interview with the elusive JT Hartley, the man who staked a claim to the biggest will of the year, only to lose the case within days. Welcome, Mr. Hartley."

Pia's jaw dropped open. This *had* to be wrong—JT hated the media. He'd never grant a television interview… would he?

The screen flicked to the guest and JT appeared, looking calm and charming, but she could see the steel in his eyes. She blinked once, then again, but he was still there on the screen. What was he doing?

"Good evening," JT said, his voice sexy-low and smooth.

"Can we start with your rumored relationship with the executor of Warner Bramson's estate? Is it true she's pregnant with your baby?"

Pia's skin chilled—why had JT opened himself, them, to *this*?

But JT seemed unruffled by the hardball question. "It's true she's pregnant," he said, gaze solemn and trustworthy, "but Pia Baxter is no longer the executor of the estate. In fact, she was fired in a case of trial by media."

The journalist's eyes became even brighter at this unexpected development. "She was fired?"

"People were concerned she may have acted unethically because of her relationship to me, but I have to tell you, Jimmy," the camera came in for a close-up on JT's unwavering eyes, "I've never met anyone in my life as principled as Pia Baxter."

"But she's pregnant, isn't she? With your baby. And you were a claimant to the will."

JT eased back in his chair, all effortless grace, seemingly in his element, but she knew this would be torture for him. "Let me give you an example. Despite our situation, when Pia found paperwork that proved Warner Bramson knew I was his son, she took that information straight to his heirs."

The journalist's eyes lit with glee. "*She's* the one who ended your claim? Robbed her own baby's father of—potentially—millions of dollars?"

JT tilted his head in assent. "It was the right thing to do. I've come to realize that Pia always does what's right, even if it's difficult, or if other people can't understand at the time."

Pia felt tears sliding down her face and absently brushed at them.

"So why are you speaking out now?" Jimmy asked. "After you've lost the claim."

JT leaned forward, as if letting Jimmy and the audience in on a secret. "To set the record straight. Pia Baxter has done the right thing, in tough circumstances, and she deserves recognition for that."

Understanding dawned and her body went limp. He was doing this for *her*. Publicly exposing himself for her career. That sweet, gorgeous fool.

The hospital room door burst open and JT strode through—tall, solid and everything she'd ever wanted. She blinked. "JT," she said, looking back to him on the screen. "But—"

Macy and April discreetly left the room. "I only just got the messages," he said as he reached her bed and grasped her hand. His hair wasn't as neat as the screen JT's, as if he'd been ploughing fingers through it, and his eyes were surrounded by tension lines. "What happened? Did you faint?"

"Cramps," she said, unable to prevent her voice from wavering. She looked down at her trembling hand as it rested on her belly. *Come on, little one, you can make it.*

JT placed a large, warm palm over her hand. "Have you seen a doctor?"

She nodded. "I haven't heard any results, though.

Dr. Crosby is on her way." His voice coming from the television drew her eyes back. "How—"

"It was taped an hour ago." His jaw clenched, then released. Clenched, then released. "I had my cell turned off for the interview and I'll never forgive myself," he said, his mouth twisting with self-recrimination.

He was beating himself up over doing something he hated for her? *Pia Baxter deserves recognition.* When she'd been searching for him, wanting him here, he'd been out trying to help her career. Everything inside her softened, and she cupped his cheek. "You didn't need to do it."

"My claim on a dead man's money has cost you too much." His voice was a rasp, his eyes tormented.

"It wasn't your fault I was fired, JT," she said, meaning every word. "*I* made those choices."

His eyes flicked to the television, where the reporter was asking a question—a grimace passed across his features and was gone in less than an instant. Then he turned back to her, expression solemn.

"I had to try and salvage your reputation. And it worked." He smiled, but it didn't reach his eyes. "I took four calls with job offers for you on the drive over here."

"Thank you, but—"

"We're a team now," he said, silencing her with a finger on her lips. "And no matter what happens today, even if it's the worst—" his voice broke on the word, and he swallowed before continuing "—this time we'll stick together. We'll get through it. Together."

She squeezed her eyes shut against the tears that threatened and tried to close her heart as well before she read too much into his words.

"No promises, JT," she whispered.

"*Yes,* princess, I'm making promises." His eyes were

solemn, intent on hers. "I love you and I won't let you go again."

The tears breached her defenses and spilled down her cheeks. These were the words her heart wanted so desperately to hear, but were they real? He thought he was losing another baby and was desperately trying to hold on. Yet now that she'd heard them, if it *was* merely his fears talking, her heart would break into a thousand pieces.

Dr. Crosby walked in through the doors, her features as unruffled as ever. "Hello, Pia. JT."

As JT tightened his grip on her hand, Pia said shakily, "Thank you for coming in."

"No trouble," Dr. Crosby said as she sank her hands into the pockets of her white coat. "I've reviewed the scans and I've spoken to the doctor who saw you when you were admitted." She smiled kindly. "We agree that the placenta is intact and your baby seems fine."

Pia shuddered as a mammoth weight on her shoulders dissolved. Her free hand curved around the small bump of her belly, caressing. *You'll be fine, little one.*

"But what about the cramps?" JT asked, pinning the doctor with his gaze. Pia stilled her hand as she looked back to the doctor.

"I can see why they would cause you concern with your history, but they were likely Braxton-Hicks, practice contractions, if you like. With the excellent care you're taking of yourself, there's every reason to believe this baby will go to term."

"Thank you," Pia whispered.

Dr. Crosby rocked forward on the balls of her feet, a twinkle in her eye. "There was extra information in the scan—would you like to know the sex of your baby?"

Pia's breath caught as she looked up at JT, who raised his eyebrows, leaving the decision to her. Her heart swelled—she wanted to know everything there was to know about their baby. She turned back to the doctor and grinned. "Yes, please."

"You're having a boy." As Dr. Cosby left the room, Pia looked down at her belly in stunned wonder. *My son.* Tears filled her eyes. *I love you, little boy.*

JT climbed onto the bed and held her close against him. "A son. We're having a son," he murmured. "Everything will be okay." His hand stroked up and down her arm, comforting.

She glanced up into JT's eyes and her mood abruptly swept down. Her son was safe, but JT... Her chest constricted, as if falling in on itself. *She might never have the only man she'd ever loved.* And now that she'd recognized that this *was* love, how could she bear to not have him? Pain exploded behind her breastbone and she edged away on the narrow bed.

"I won't hold you to what you said before," she said quietly.

His forehead creased into a frown. "About not letting you go again? I meant that."

"I know you meant it—" she moistened her dry lips "—but it was a natural reaction, just your fear speaking. Everything's fine with the baby, so we can go back to the way we were." She would *never* keep him to words he'd spoken in desperation.

JT lifted himself up on an elbow. His gaze met hers as his Adam's apple bobbed down, then up.

"Pia, I'll be brutally honest," he said, eyes clear and unguarded. "You broke my heart fourteen years ago, but I now know why you had to—you were so young, barely more than a child, and you were grieving. You had to do it for your own survival." His voice was smooth, tender, containing no judgment. But regret for how she'd handled things over the years rose in her.

"I wish I could—"

Softly, he kissed away the rest of her words, then drew back, smiling crookedly at her. "And for *my* survival, I had to smother my love. It never faltered, even for a *second,* but I couldn't risk the pain, so I hid it. Including from myself. Even recently, spending time together again, I told myself I couldn't open my heart to you or the baby, that I'd be crushed if you left or something happened to our child."

"Life doesn't have any guarantees, JT," she said softly. A tear slipped down her cheek. Why had it always been so impossible for them? He still loved her, he admitted it, but he would never open his heart fully again and that would kill any love they had, any relationship they formed.

Vibrant green eyes sparkled at her through dark lashes. "Tell me, what do you think of the name Thomas?"

Everything inside her stilled as she understood his meaning—he was *planning ahead.* "You're willing to choose a name?" she asked, breathless.

Gently, he smoothed a wisp of hair behind her ears and kissed her forehead. "I've discovered something—the greatest things in life need the greatest risk. And I'm prepared to risk everything for you and our son. I love you both."

Happiness washed over her in waves too large to withstand—her heart was filled to bursting point, her body wracked with trembling joy. Wrapping her arms around his shoulders, she clung to him and surrendered to the majesty of the moment.

"I love you, too," she finally said through the tears that clogged her throat. She looked up and met his gaze. "More than I ever have before. More than I thought was possible."

He pulled her into a fierce embrace, and as she laid her

head against his chest, she felt all the air leave his lungs in one long breath. *He'd been nervous,* she realized and held back a fresh round of tears.

She pulled back and held his face between both her hands. "JT, I promise I'll never shut you out again," she vowed.

He kissed her lightly on the lips, then smiled his crooked smile. "And I promise I'll never give up on us."

Epilogue

Pia stood in the foyer of the Lighthouse Hotel, surrounded by her two sisters, April Fairchild—now a good friend and soon-to-be sister-in-law—and Theresa Hartley. Their love swirled around her as richly as her cream wedding gown. She bent down to kiss the top of her baby boy's head. Thomas's strawberry blond hair was cool and silky under her lips.

"You be good for Nana," she told the eight-month-old.

Theresa hugged the baby tight and smiled at Pia with tears in her eyes. "He's always a good boy for me, aren't you, Tommy?"

Pia's sisters gave Thomas a quick kiss as well before Pia waved goodbye and Theresa Hartley left with the baby to take her seat outside under the marquee. Seth and April's hotel had closed to the public this weekend for the family event, so the only people onsite were family, friends and the staff preparing for the reception in the ballroom.

April stepped forward, looking every inch the superstar, with her caramel-and-honey hair styled and glossy, her matching caramel eyes bright. "I think I'd better go and take my place now, too. Are you sure there's nothing you want before I go?"

"No, I'll be fine." Pia said, squeezing April's hand. "My sisters are here and Macy will be back in a moment."

April kissed Pia's cheek. "You look beautiful. JT will be knocked out when he sees you."

Pia smiled, still not quite believing she was acquiring such a large and wonderful new family through this marriage.

As April left, she passed Macy coming the other way, and they paused for a brief hug. Macy grasped Pia's hand when she reached her.

"Every time I see you in that dress, I'm impressed all over again that you made it yourself." Macy looked down at her own dress and across at Pia's sisters. "Or these dresses. They're stunning."

The dresses had turned out even better than Pia had imagined. She'd wanted the three bridesmaids and April in blues and greens to harmonize with the sky, trees and ocean around the hotel, and had made a light, almost transparent overlay that would move with the sea breeze. Every stitch was from her own hand, and had allowed for lots of bonding time with her new sisters-in-law during fittings, which was a better outcome than the dresses themselves. And they'd discussed her ideas for a little store that sold Pia Baxter originals—with Macy's business brain and April's contacts, it was off to a great start.

Macy exchanged greetings with Pia's sisters, then turned back to Pia. "I've settled Georgia down with Ryder's mother. She's sitting with Theresa, so the babies can see each other." She looked pensively toward the doorway.

"You were right, you know. Those babies are healing the harsh feelings."

Pia's heart filled with even more joy. "I'm so glad." It helped that Ryder's mother had never heard of Theresa until the past year, so had no built-up animosity. She'd even told Pia she felt bad for what Theresa had gone through at her husband's hand, and they now had a tentative friendship. Pia had invited them all today—every member of her new, unconventional family, and they'd all accepted.

"It might take a bit longer for Seth's and Ryder's mothers to settle their differences," Macy said, "but they've come a long way already to both be at this ceremony."

Pia's eldest sister popped her head out the door in the direction of the marquee. "They're getting April ready. I think it's almost our cue."

"Nervous?" Macy asked.

"Yes," Pia said, holding up her trembling hand. "I don't know why, though, I can barely wait to marry that man."

"I was nervous when I married Ryder, too." A faraway expression drifted across Macy's face—she was obviously remembering that day. "I think it's just because we want everything to go perfectly, and the excitement."

The string quartet started to play, then April's voice floated on the air in a sweet melody. Pia's sisters gave her a quick hug, then walked out the door, bouquets at chest height, and proceeded toward the marquee. Heart racing, Pia watched them go and clutched tighter to her own posy of bright purple blooms.

Macy tossed her a broad smile, then followed the other women out the door.

"I thought they'd never leave." The deep voice that came from the shadows made her shiver.

"I wondered when you would show up," she said as she

turned to the man she loved with all her heart. "You're cutting it close."

He grinned his crooked grin as he slipped an arm around her waist. "Somehow I don't think they'll start without us."

They'd decided to walk up the aisle together, starting their marriage side by side, just as they intended to live it, but seeing him standing in front of her in his three-piece suit, she wondered at the wisdom of their choice—she just wanted to melt into him, not walk outside.

She took a deep breath, hoping it would restore sanity. "Maybe not, but April is out there singing the song she wrote for us," she said, her heart skipping a beat as he leaned in, his breath warm on her face.

"And we don't want to deprive the audience from hearing it in its entirety." He feathered a kiss across her lips.

Sanity fled. "You make a good point." She pulled him close, her breathing ragged. "But we also don't want to mess up my lipstick just before our own wedding."

"You can fix it for the photos," he murmured, a breath away from her lips.

Pia looked into his beautiful, vibrant green eyes and examined her choices—to walk up the aisle with lipstick on her lips, or with the taste of JT on them. Not a hard decision when put like that. She twined her arms around his neck and captured his mouth. But before the kiss could become heated, the sound of someone clearing their throat brought her back to her senses. She dragged her mouth away from JT's and looked up to find the hotel's manager, Oscar, delicately staring down at his shoes.

"Now might be a good time," Oscar said, diplomatically. "Before April runs out of words to sing."

Pia laughed as she wiped her thumb over JT's sensual lips, removing any trace of her pink lipstick.

"Thank you, Oscar," JT said, then turned to Pia. "Shall we?"

"Love to," she said, and they walked to the door and out over the grass, hands firmly grasped together.

The snowy white marquee was bursting with people on white chairs with bows at the back. Her mother and father watched her from the front row, much happier that she was marrying a wealthy property developer than they'd ever been about her relationship with a teenage boy from the wrong side of the tracks. Any final resistance had melted when they first held Thomas. Beside her parents were her sisters' husbands, who were surrounded by their children. Pia smiled at them, then blew a kiss to Thomas, snug in Theresa's arms, who waved his fists in the air when he caught sight of his parents.

"As gorgeous as his mother," JT whispered as he threw their son a broad smile.

Up ahead, at the end of the aisle, Pia's sisters and Macy were on one side, and Ryder, Seth and JT's attorney, Philip Hendricks, on the other. In the year since she'd called JT's half brothers to that meeting, a slow-growing bond had been developing between the three men. They weren't yet golfing buddies, but they could hold a conversation and share a joke. She—along with April and Macy—had high hopes for what the future would bring the brothers.

JT paused and turned her to him. "I just want you to know," he said, the love in his eyes unmasked, "I love you, princess. I've always loved you." He pulled her hands to cover his chest. "You're my heart."

She pressed her lips together in an attempt to stem the tears that threatened, but one slipped out and JT brushed it from her cheek. Then she gave up fighting an unwinnable war and let the others follow the path of the first. "I love you, too, JT Hartley. And I know with everything inside me, this love will keep growing forever."

Then in front of their friends and family, before they'd even made it to the top of the aisle, JT hauled her against him and kissed his bride.

* * * * *

COMING NEXT MONTH

Available November 8, 2011

#2119 WANTED BY HER LOST LOVE
Maya Banks
Pregnancy & Passion

#2120 TEMPTATION
Brenda Jackson
Texas Cattleman's Club: The Showdown

#2121 NOTHING SHORT OF PERFECT
Day Leclaire
Billionaires and Babies

#2122 RECLAIMING HIS PREGNANT WIDOW
Tessa Radley

#2123 IMPROPERLY WED
Anna DePalo

#2124 THE PRICE OF HONOR
Emilie Rose

HDCNM1011

Harlequin® Special Edition® is thrilled to present a new installment in USA TODAY *bestselling author RaeAnne Thayne's reader-favorite miniseries,* THE COWBOYS OF COLD CREEK.

Join the excitement as we meet the Bowmans—four siblings who lost their parents but keep family ties alive in Pine Gulch. First up is Trace. Only two things get under this rugged lawman's skin: beautiful women and secrets. And in Rebecca Parsons, he finds both!

Read on for a sneak peek of CHRISTMAS IN COLD CREEK. Available November 2011 from Harlequin® Special Edition®.

On impulse, he unfolded himself from the bar stool. "Need a hand?"

"Thank you! I..." She lifted her gaze from the floor to his jeans and then raised her eyes. When she identified him her hazel eyes turned from grateful to unfriendly and cold, as if he'd somehow thrown the broken glasses at her head.

He also thought he saw a glimmer of panic in those interesting depths, which instantly stirred his curiosity like cream swirling through coffee.

"I've got it, Officer. Thank you." Her voice was several degrees colder than the whirl of sleet outside the windows.

Despite her protests, he knelt down beside her and began to pick up shards of broken glass. "No problem. Those trays can be slippery."

This close, he picked up the scent of her, something fresh and flowery that made him think of a mountain meadow on a July afternoon. She had a soft, lush mouth and for one brief, insane moment, he wanted to push aside that stray lock of hair slipping from her ponytail and taste her. Apparently he needed to spend a lot less time working and a great deal *more* time recreating with the opposite sex if he could have sudden random fantasies about a woman he wasn't even inclined to like, pretty or not.

"I'm Trace Bowman. You must be new in town."

She didn't answer immediately and he could almost see the wheels turning in her head. Why the hesitancy? And why that little hint of unease he could see clouding the edge of her gaze? His presence was obviously making her uncomfortable and Trace couldn't help wondering why.

"Yes. We've been here a few weeks."

"Well, I'm just up the road about four lots, in the white house with the cedar shake roof, if you or your daughter need anything." He smiled at her as he picked up the last shard of glass and set it on her tray.

Definitely a story there, he thought as she hurried away. He just might need to dig a little into her background to find out why someone with fine clothes and nice jewelry, and who so obviously didn't have experience as a waitress, would be here slinging hash at The Gulch. Was she running away from someone? A bad marriage?

So…Rebecca Parsons. Not Becky. An intriguing woman. It had been a long time since one of those had crossed his path here in Pine Gulch.

Trace won't rest until he finds out Rebecca's secret, but will he still have that same attraction to her once he does? Find out in CHRISTMAS IN COLD CREEK. Available November 2011 from Harlequin® Special Edition®.

HSEEXP1111